Copyright © 2024 by Lexa M. Mack

Published by Indies United Publishing House, LLC
First Edition published February 2024

Edited by Meredith Phillips

Cover art designed by Tatiana Villa

This is a work of fiction. The names, characters, businesses, places, events and incidents are either the products of the author's imagination or used in a fictitious manner.

All rights reserved worldwide. No part of this publication may be replicated, redistributed, or given away in any form without the prior written consent of the author and/or publisher.

ISBN: 978-1-64456-697-8 [Paperback]
ISBN: 978-1-64456-698-5 [Mobi]
ISBN: 978-1-64456-699-2 [ePub]

Library of Congress Control Number: 2023952326

INDIES UNITED PUBLISHING HOUSE, LLC
P.O. BOX 3071
QUINCY, IL 62305-3071
www.indiesunited.net

LITANY OF LIES

SFUndertheRug.com Series
Book Two

Lexa M. Mack

INDIES UNITED PUBLISHING HOUSE, LLC

CHAPTER ONE

Beatrice struggled to unlock the door to the stately home on Walnut Street. Lashing wind blew up the edge of her raincoat and freezing rain seeped under the hood covering her mass of beaded braids. A trickle of icy water slid down the front of her dress. As a child in Jamaica, she'd danced and played under the weeping heavens but living in San Francisco had cured her of her love of rain. At least it didn't snow here. Beatrice had only seen snow during the annual jaunts to the house in Sugar Bowl for skiing when she'd worked for the Spencer family. Other than trekking from the car to the cabin and back she'd never ventured out into it and had no desire to. Finally, the heavy door swung open and she stumbled inside.

She felt guilty when she spent a night away. She didn't like to leave Ms. Gardner alone for very long. "Greta," she whispered. It was hard to call her employer by her first name, though the woman insisted.

She was returning later than she'd intended. The quick breakfast with

Kestrel Jonas had lasted much longer than expected. Kestrel had been especially entertaining and the bottomless mimosas hadn't helped any. Kestrel's blog, *SFUndertheRug.com*, was about to break the underground story of the year, and Beatrice had been her best source.

She noticed that the boxes of Christmas ornaments her employer had insisted on locating in the dusty attic and dragging down the ladder still sat untouched in the entry. Well, she would help get them up this week. It was good that Greta felt well enough to decorate for the holidays.

Leaving her dripping raincoat hanging on the antique coat tree she scooped up yesterday's mail from the tiled floor and placed it on the mirrored entry table. Trundling her wheelie bag back to her quarters she decided she would pop a quick coffee cake into the oven before going upstairs. The recipe was one of Greta's favorites; one her mother had made when she was a child. Rich with sour cream, the cardamom swirls of streusel running through the batter and on top of the cake were a Gardner family secret.

Once the cake was in the oven Beatrice gathered up the mail, made her way up the steep stairs, and knocked gently on the bedroom door. It was early, Greta must still be sleeping. She quietly opened the door. The older woman was not in the bed nor in the ornate armchair beside the window where she sometimes worked on her crossword puzzles. The room was dim, and the only sound was the slashing rain outside. She stepped to the bedside table and turned off the lamp. The bathroom door was closed. Maybe Greta was taking a bath, although a morning bath would be unusual. She always said, "Showers in the morning and baths at night."

Beatrice crossed the room and knocked lightly on the bathroom door. "Greta, are you in there" No sound came from inside and she tapped a little harder. "Greta, are you okay?"

Anxious now, she slowly opened the door. She noted the familiar mixed scents of bath salts and incense, but there was a sharper smell beneath that. The candles on the side of the tub had burned down. Greta was there, below the water, her wispy gray hair billowed out around her face and her gaunt body looked tiny and pale in the thin light from the window.

"Oh, my God. Oh, my God. Greta, Greta…" She rushed to the side of the tub and stood wringing her hands. She could see there was nothing to be done. She couldn't think. She'd have to call the police. She hated to leave Greta there, under the water, but everyone knew you weren't supposed to touch anything. But was that only if someone was murdered? What if someone just died. Maybe had a heart attack or a stroke, and drowned? Or died in their bed, in their sleep. Should she try to get her out of the tub? Maybe she wasn't really dead, maybe she could be revived.

Beatrice ran into the bedroom and looked around for Greta's cell phone. It was there on the nightstand, plugged into the charger the way it would have been any night before she went to sleep. Beatrice grabbed it up and dialed 9-1-1.

The call was answered immediately, "Hello, this is the 911 operator, what is the nature of your emergency?"

"It's Ms. Gardner, she's dead. I just found her here…dead."

"Are you certain that the person is dead? How did you determine they are dead?"

"She's in the bathtub…under the water…not moving."

"Are you calling to report a suspicious death?"

"I don't think so. Just a death. She's dead." Beatrice could hear her voice rising as she spoke. She just wanted this magical person at the end of the line, to *do* something.

"I'll dispatch an officer to the address. If it seems to be a natural death it may not have priority over other current calls."

"Oh, I guess that makes sense. But can you please hurry?"

"Yes, ma'am, please give me some information and do not touch or move anything on the scene. What is your address?"

What was the address? Suddenly Beatrice's mind went blank. She could remember her address on Victoria Street in Jamaica when she was a child but the number on Walnut Street completely left her mind. "I don't know. I can't remember the number. It's the third house from California Street. It's gray with dark blue trim…and white. Some white trim. Wait, I remember, it is 504 Walnut Street."

"Is that in San Francisco?"

"Yes, in San Francisco. 504 Walnut Street."

"Could I please have your name."

"Yes, my name is Beatrice Campbell."

"Are you a family member of the deceased, Ms. Campbell?"

"No, I'm just…" What was she? She and Greta had laughed about how to describe her role to people. "I'm her companion. Not a partner; like a housekeeper or caregiver."

"I'll dispatch someone to that address. Can I call you back on this number, if necessary?"

"Yes, it's her cell phone. I'll keep it with me."

"Please try to relax, ma'am. Someone will be there shortly. I will ask them to call you when they are on their way."

"Okay, okay, I'll keep the phone with me."

Beatrice sat for several minutes on the edge of the bed. She didn't want to go back into the bathroom, but she didn't like to leave Greta alone in there.

Suddenly she remembered her coffee cake and went down the stairs to check on it. She turned on the kettle and started to make a pot of tea in the Brown Betty pot she and Greta always used, the one Greta had brought back from England after her first honeymoon. She put the pot down and just dropped a teabag into a mug. She'd suddenly realized she and Greta would never be sharing a pot of tea again, and it seemed so very sad.

When she'd pulled the coffee cake from the oven and set it on a rack to cool, she sat by the kitchen window letting her tea get cold and wondering what she was supposed to do. The house felt oddly chill and when the old building creaked, as it often did, she jumped and turned, almost expecting Greta to come through the door. When the cell phone in her pocket rang she didn't realize what it was at first but finally grabbed it on the third ring.

"Hello, hello. Ms. Gardner's phone."

"Hello, ma'am. This is Inspector Bobby Burns from the San Francisco Police Department. I'm in your neighborhood and got a call that someone has died at your address and that you are distraught."

"Yes, someone is dead, and yes, I am distraught."

Bobby laughed to himself. The situation wasn't funny, but the comment was, kind of. "Your address is 504 Walnut Street. Is that correct?"

"Yes, 504 Walnut Street."

"Okay, I'm a couple of blocks away and I will probably get there before the coroner. Can you have someone be there to let me in?"

"Yes, I can let you in. I am the only one here." Beatrice knew there was no reason to be nervous, but the last time she'd had to call someone because of a death, it had been such a risk, such an important thing. She couldn't help but think back to it. Her Auntie Bea had died. It was not unexpected, she'd been very sick, and Beatrice was only twenty years old and all alone with her. They had no friends yet in San Francisco. The coroner had come, everything had been fine, but her life had changed forever that day.

CHAPTER TWO

Inspector Burns parked his car at the curb and looked around the neighborhood. It was a nice, upscale San Francisco street. Far better than he would ever be able to afford. He'd been looking around for a bigger place, not that he could ever buy here. Bay Area real estate was not something for the working man, even a working man and woman together. He was thinking of asking Rocky to move in with him, maybe even thinking about getting married, but they wouldn't be moving to this end of town.

The woman who answered the door looked vaguely familiar. She was tall and slim and her long, beaded braids were caught up in a bundle at the back of her head.

"I'm Inspector Burns, and you are?"

"I am Beatrice, Beatrice Campbell. I am… was, Ms. Gardner's companion. Please come in."

Before Bobby could even get through the door Beatrice was halfway up the stairs. "She's up here. She must have drowned or had a heart attack or something. She's been sick but I thought she was better...." Her final words were lost to him as she went through the bedroom door and he followed behind her up the stairs.

When he went into the bedroom the woman had stopped at another door on the other side of the room. "I didn't touch anything in there. I hated to just leave her there but I could see that she was gone."

Bobby stepped past her and went into the bathroom. He too, could see that the woman was gone. He also didn't touch anything. "Can you tell me what the scents in this room are? Are they familiar?"

"Yes, well mostly they are. There are the candles that burnt down and the bath salts that Greta used, and then the incense. The cones are in that jar at the end of the tub."

"Is that all?"

"No, there is some other smell in here that I don't recognize, but I don't know what it is."

"OK, well, someone from the coroner's office should be here soon, so let's go back downstairs and you can tell me how you found her."

Beatrice looked relieved to have someone else telling her what she should do. She had not gone back into the bathroom and stood in the doorway taking one last shuddering glance at what used to be her friend.

Beatrice led Bobby downstairs into the living room. "Do you want some coffee or tea or anything?"

"No thank you, Ms. Campbell. But get something yourself if you like."

Beatrice eyed the bottle of bourbon on the drinks trolley but turned away.

Bobby sat in the wing backed chair facing the fabulous view of the bay with the heavy clouds darkening the water, and Beatrice sat on the edge of the love seat.

"So, what caused you to be here this morning, Ms. Campbell?"

"Please call me Beatrice. Ms. Campbell just doesn't sound right. I was here this morning because I live here with Ms. Gardner. I am her live-in companion since she became ill some months ago."

"Would you normally go into Ms. Gardner's bathroom in the morning?"

"No, I was not here yesterday nor last night as it was my day off. I returned this morning. I used to not go away on the weekends when Greta was so sick, but she'd been feeling better and said she'd be fine. I should never have left her here alone. Maybe this wouldn't have happened if I'd come home last night..."

Bobby waited patiently for her to finish. It was not unusual for someone under stress to give you a lot more information than you asked for. As a homicide detective it usually worked in your favor. In this case, he just happened to be the closest policeman to the scene, so he'd stepped in on a Sunday morning.

It must have been a slow day for unexpected death in San Francisco as the coroner's van pulled into the driveway about half an hour after Bobby arrived.

When he saw the vehicle pull up Bobby stood and Beatrice turned to the window. "Oh my, Greta would hate them to park in the driveway. Do they have to do that?"

"Yes, ma'am. They are going to be bringing in some equipment and will eventually remove the body, so they need to be as close as possible."

"Of course."

Bobby went to the front door and let Dr. Kirschman in. Another police car had pulled up in front of the house and two beefy police officers followed the coroner through the door.

"Good morning, Inspector Burns. I'm surprised to see you here. I understood that this is an accidental death."

"It is as far as I know, but I happened to be in the area, so I took the call." Once again, Bobby was unnerved by the cheerful energy and youthful looks of the coroner. "I'm surprised to see you on a Sunday, as well."

"No rest for the wicked, they say." She laughed lightly as she followed him up the stairs to Greta's room. Bobby had taken the coroner out for drinks a couple of times, but her quirky cheerfulness and dark humor had put him off. It was just weird that the woman spent her life examining dead bodies.

Bobby glanced around the bedroom. It was always strange to be looking with a careful eye at the belongings and detritus of a person who was dead; the half-drunk cup of cold tea, a plate with a few cookie crumbs, the used tissue left crumpled on the bedside table. Now the person was gone and before long all those bits of their last minutes would also be gone. Still, it was his job to be observant. He saw that she'd had a snack, set out her robe, left her laptop open on the bed. Out here, nothing looking especially out of place. He reached out with his gloved finger and touched the computer to life. *SFUndertheRug.com*, the hugely popular society gossip blog, popped onto the screen. "Figures," he muttered.

Dr. Kirschman stepped to the bathroom door. "I have some questions for the person who discovered the body. Are they available?"

"Sure, I'll ask her to come up." Bobby stepped out the bedroom door. One of the officers stood in the hallway. "Could you please have Ms. Campbell come upstairs? The coroner has some questions."

The smell of sweet baked goods and coffee wafted up the stairwell. "What's going on down there?"

"The lady had just baked a fresh cake this morning and made us a pot of coffee." The man's voice was muffled from scarfing down his last bite of cake. Crumbs speckled the carpet beneath his feet.

Beatrice entered the bedroom cautiously.

Bobby escorted her to the bathroom door. "Dr. Kirschman, this is Ms. Campbell. She was the deceased's paid companion and discovered the body this morning when she returned from her day off. Is that correct, Ms. Campbell?"

"Yes, that's right. I had stayed with my girls...with some friends, last night instead of coming home." Her voice trembled slightly. "I should have come home last night. Maybe she would be okay."

The coroner hesitated. "Now, now...I just have a few questions. Can you identify these various bath items and tell me if you see anything unusual or out of place?" Bobby had noticed before now that the coroner, as cheerful and competent as she was, sometimes seemed more comfortable with the dead than she was with the living.

Beatrice stepped into the room, averting her eyes from the body. The doctor had already taken samples of the bath water and drained the tub. She'd also draped one of the luxurious towels over the body, not disturbing anything in the process.

"These are Greta's, Ms. Gardner's, usual bath items. She loved a fancy bath to relax." Beatrice pointed at individual items on the ledge around the huge, jetted tub. "These are the bath oils, salts, and bath bombs that she liked. She always had candles around the tub and the lights turned off. All of these candles have burned down, though. That jar has incense cones in it, and that is the incense burner she always used. The Aladdin's lamp brass thing there. She always coordinated the scents, lavender or rose or honeysuckle; bubbles, candles, and incense."

Dr. Kirschman had picked up the incense burner carefully with her gloved hands. "What scent did she use last night, do you think?"

"Lavender, I think. The candles were purple, and it still smells of them in here."

The coroner lifted the lid of the incense burner and sniffed, then held it out to Beatrice. "Is this what the lavender incense usually smells like?"

Beatrice leaned forward and sniffed the burner. "Not really, that smells stronger, but it might be because she'd been using that burner for years and years. Decades. She told me she got it at Cost Plus when she was a teenager, in the sixties, and she'd used it ever since."

"Is there anything missing from the bathroom that you would have expected to see here?"

Beatrice glanced around the room. "No, there's even the split of champagne and flute she would bring in with her. She said it made the bath perfect."

"All right, Ms. Campbell. Thanks for your help. One more thing… did you touch or move anything in here or in the bedroom when you came in this morning?"

"No, ma'am. I just opened the door to the bedroom, turned off the lamp, and then walked across to the bathroom door and knocked when I saw she wasn't in bed."

"Thank you."

"Wait, I did use Greta's cell phone to call the police. I have it here." She drew the phone from her pocket. "It was plugged into the charger next to the bed when I came in."

When Beatrice left, Dr. Kirschman turned to Bobby. "It turns out to be serendipitous that you came this morning, Inspector Burns. You are going to need to call in a Crime Scene Team, I don't think this was an accidental death."

CHAPTER THREE

Six weeks earlier...

Beatrice struggled through the massive door with her various bags and bundles. The Spencers had always ordered their grocery deliveries online or had the cook do the shopping, but Greta Gardner liked to have things done her own way and she paid Beatrice well to make sure that happened. In this case it meant trekking all over the city to various specialty stores on a regular basis. Greta insisted that this was how things were done in Europe. The main difference was that the traffic and parking hurdles to doing it that way in a city like San Francisco added a lot of hassle to the process. There was a bakery for bread made with a sourdough mother from 150 years ago, the special cookies she loved from a tiny bakery near Civic Center, organic produce from Green Earth on Divisadero, cheeses from Cowgirl Creamery at the Ferry Building; at least the meat market was in the same building and it was near Fisherman's Wharf where you could get the freshest fish, right off the boat. The list went on, but for today Beatrice had thrown in the rain-soggy towel before getting to the Wine Exchange on Taylor Street.

Heaving the bags up onto the immaculate, though dated, tile counter in the kitchen she thought of how little Greta ate anymore. The cancer that was ravaging her body combined with the chemotherapy meant that, even though Beatrice did her best to tempt her, Greta ate very little. However, what little she ate was of the best quality.

Before she put things away Beatrice would go up the long flight of stairs and check on the frail woman who lay in that huge bed that looked likely to swallow her up at any moment.

Beatrice would take up a cup of tea, the newspaper, the latest mail, and a tiny plate with a few of the delicate macarons she'd bought. Greta said they reminded her of France and she would smile and nibble on one until Beatrice went back downstairs and she could fall asleep with the television murmuring in the background.

Halfway up the stairs Beatrice was surprised to hear muffled voices from the bedroom followed by Greta's light laugh and a deeper chuckle. The bedroom door was ajar and she turned, pushing it open with her hip as she entered carrying the tea tray.

Greta had transformed while Beatrice was gone. Her sparse hair had been combed and caught up with a clip at the nape of her neck. She was wearing the quilted satin bed jacket that someone had sent her a few weeks ago and that she had flung to the side as too silly and frivolous for lying around in bed. It was hard to tell if the pink in her cheeks was from a touch of makeup or a girlish blush, but the carefully applied lip color was definitely from a tube.

Both Greta and the man seated in the chair next to her bed were startled from their laughter by Beatrice's entrance but then they gave each other devilish grins and burst into another peal of laughter.

"My goodness Ms. Gardner, you two seem to be having a wonderful time. Hello, Mr. Frankel. I didn't know you were coming or I would have put my shopping off until later."

"Beatrice, dear, Bertie didn't need you to hang around. He's had a key to this house for forty years. Had to have it to help me up the stairs after those wild parties, didn't you, Bertie?"

Bertram Frankel had stopped laughing but a smile still lingered around his mouth, not really reaching his eyes. "Yes, darling, those were the days." He sat stolidly in the fragile chair with his beringed fingers folded over his ample waistcoat. To Beatrice he always looked like he was dressed up for a fancy party; no jeans or khakis for him, always waistcoats and bow ties.

She turned to place the heavy tray on the table by the window and noted the empty bottle of champagne in the wastebasket. There were two empty glasses on the bedside table where the pill bottles usually stood. It looked as though Greta had swept the medications into the drawer when she'd learned Bertie was on his way.

Having company initially gave Greta a lift, but the toll taken by getting up from her bed, dressing, and then entertaining a guest, would be felt later with a restless night and an exhausted next day.

But it wasn't Beatrice's place to decide what Ms. Gardner should or shouldn't be doing. She was paid to help her with whatever she needed. Still, she'd grown fond of the little woman in the past few months and, from the stories Beatrice had heard Greta tell, she wasn't always the best judge of what was good for her.

Beatrice turned back to the bed. "You probably aren't really in the mood for tea and cookies, but I could bring up some of those cheese straws I made yesterday and some charcuterie, if you would like a bit of something before dinner."

Greta started to decline but Bertie broke in. "What is for dinner this evening, Beatrice?"

"Well, I wasn't really expecting company, but if you want to have a snack now, I can serve you something more substantial in about an hour." Her mind was ticking off the list of suitable items she'd bought today along with what was still in the pantry.

Beatrice was a good cook of plain food and had learned how to prepare the special dishes that Greta sometimes requested, and then hardly ate a bite of. Beatrice really cooked for one and ate the food that Greta did not, even though the rich dishes did not always agree with her.

"Don't look so worried, I'm not really going to stay for dinner." Bertie turned to Greta and patted the hand that lay on top of the bedspread. "I have a dinner at the PU Club tonight, but I will come another night and sample Beatrice's cooking."

Why was it that Beatrice always felt that Bertie was making fun of her in that smug, supercilious manner of his? He acted as if he didn't like her, although she couldn't imagine why. But it didn't really matter, as she didn't like him either. Still, it was nice of him to come visit his old friend. As Greta had gotten sicker her friends had come by less and less.

Fewer of them came, they came less often, and they stayed for shorter visits. Beatrice thought it was sad that people disappeared into the woodwork when you really needed them.

By the time her visitor was ready to depart, the pink in Greta's cheeks had gone gray and she could hardly keep her eyes open. Beatrice escorted Bertie to the door and bolted it behind him. She couldn't help but wonder how many keys to this house Greta had handed out over her lifetime.

Bertie had called an Uber for a ride, as he didn't like to drive in the city, especially at night. His driver would deliver him to the front doors of the Pacific Union Club, where only the elite members could enter and he would join the rest of the old, white men and their guests for an elaborate dinner. The PU club perched regally at the top of Nob Hill between Grace Cathedral and the Fairmont Hotel. Some said between the sacred and the profane. The building that was originally the Flood Mansion had survived the 1906 earthquake and most of the incursions of the twenty-first century. Membership was still male only, expensive, and very select.

Upstairs, Beatrice helped Greta out of the bed jacket, adjusted her pillows, dispensed her medications, and asked what she'd like for dinner.

"Oh, I don't know, maybe just some soup, something light. Maybe toast. I'm sure whatever you make will be fine. Let me just rest here for a bit."

"Yes, Ms. Gardner. I'll just lower this light and bring something up in a while."

Going downstairs with the tea tray Beatrice thought what a murderous, unrelenting thing cancer was. You started out hopeful when you first got the diagnosis, then you got treated nearly to death.

CHAPTER FOUR

Bertie bustled down the steps in the downpour and hopped into the Uber car waiting on the street. He had been known to turn down rides in tiny cars with male drivers he found menacing, but today the ride would be short and he was running late for his dinner. He sighed recalling the days of rides in town cars with liveried drivers who opened the door for him and were not annoyingly listening to radio stations broadcasting in languages he didn't speak, which would be all languages other than English.

He had already checked out the evening's menu on the message he received from the club and was anxious to partake of the first Dungeness crab of the season. The California Dungeness crab season usually began in early November, and it often coincided with his regularly scheduled monthly meeting with his cadre of school friends. In this case he wasn't necessarily talking about college, as most of these men were "of an age," and had been in school together since their nannies had escorted them to their elite pre-schools. If Bertie had cared to, he could have located the picture of all of them lined up in their short pants at three years of age. Maybe he would see if he could find the photo before the December gala luncheon.

Rather than having his driver drop him off in front of the impressive building at 1000 California Street, he directed him to the back entrance. It was easier to duck in the back way in the rain. Besides, there were no tourists to impress with his entrance.

A number of people had gathered for drinks in the foyer, and he spied his little knot of friends standing near the bar and joined them after procuring his first official libation of the evening. The champagne he'd shared with Greta had worn off by now, and he was losing that lovely glow he tried to maintain during all of his waking hours. If he timed it right, Bloody Mary's or Screwdrivers with breakfast, wine with lunch, a few pre-dinner aperitifs and more wine with dinner could keep him in a steady state of inebriation. Never really drunk, but never really sober, either.

"Evening, Bertie. How are you?" The first person who greeted him was the one he wanted most to avoid. Carlton Drummond had been his financial adviser for forty years and had made him a ton of money but had lately been leaving annoying messages about reallocating his investments and the singular lack of growth in his portfolio. Bertie was not careful with money and preferred not to think of it. He'd always had it and being pushed to consider it in any serious way was disturbing. Over the past few years, he'd gotten a bit adventurous; the dot-com losses still rankled. Damned technology. Bertie liked to think of himself as more forward- thinking and hip than this bunch of stodgy classmates. It was hellish getting older and having to be more sedate and conservative. Unless you were talking about politics, of course. You could never be too conservative in that area.

"I'm doing great, Carl. Just came from visiting Greta. Hold on just a moment, I have to catch someone before they duck out of sight." With that Bertie strode away in the direction of one of the banquet rooms, leaving Carl, mouth still agape.

When they entered the dining room, *en masse*, Bertie made sure to stay clear of his adviser and sat at a table as far removed as possible. He was pretty happy to have landed a nice spot between a couple of squash-playing buddies and across from the seriously enhanced décolleté of Millie Pierce, the younger partner of one of his classmates.

He felt he'd gotten another break when he realized that one of his favorite servers, the one most likely to notice his empty wineglass, was serving his table.

The conversation over dinner was lively. Most of it concerned those of their friends and acquaintances who were not in attendance tonight. It was depressing how often the discussion veered to the illness or recent demise of someone they all knew. Tonight, one of the more titillating subjects was whether or not Hyatt Scott would marry his longtime partner, Louise, now that his wife had died. Hyatt and Louise had been living together for years and it seemed ridiculous to think it mattered at this point, but in this particular crowd, especially among the women, it mattered a great deal to be elevated to the role of wife rather than companion. The table seemed evenly split about whether or not Hyatt and Louise would tie the knot, and there was no dearth of catty remarks and witty references.

Bertie was glad that he had managed to avoid remarrying after his one ill-fated marriage had ended in divorce. Of course, he was considered quite the hot commodity in his circle and he received endless dinner invitations coupling him with every unattached woman of-an-age in the upper ranks of San Francisco. He could have his pick although the aging of his social group had reminded him of the adage about finding a husband in Alaska. "The odds are good, but the goods are odd."

At the end of the evening, standing in the foyer, Bertie was considering whether or not he should book one of the upstairs rooms at the club. He had been considerably over-served and might need help getting up the stairs.

"Bertie, how did you get here tonight? Do you need a ride home?"

Damn, it was Carlton again. "That would be great, Carl, under one condition." Bertie held up his index finger to make his point. "No talking about finances."

"All right. Have it your way, but you are going to have to talk to me sooner or later."

"Well, later works for me."

Kestrel watched the last of the diners straggle out of the dining room and off to their various destinations. Some of them who lived further away had booked rooms upstairs for the night, and she saw more than one being tactfully escorted up the stairs.

She saw Mr. Frankel stumble and right himself on his way to the parking lot, with Mr. Drummond holding his elbow to steady him. Bertram Frankel was one of her favorite guests. She kept his wineglass filled and he kept her supplied with carelessly dropped bits of information about his intimate friends. He would no doubt be surprised that he was one of the most prolific sources of information for her blog, *SFUndertheRug.com*. This evening alone he had unknowingly updated her on the status of several relationships, a possible lawsuit, and named a the heretofore mystery man in a contentious divorce, and all without actually speaking directly to her, other than thanking her for refilling his glass.

CHAPTER FIVE

On Walnut Street Beatrice was shutting the house down for the evening. She'd managed to get Greta to eat a few sips of chicken soup, the nourishing Caribbean recipe she'd grown up on, though she'd toned down the spiciness for Greta's palate.

Over the months that she'd worked there they had developed a habit of taking tea and chatting together before bed while Greta's medications kicked in. Sometimes Greta would read or play on her iPhone. Other times she'd talk of her life growing up in San Francisco or even ask Beatrice questions about life in Jamaica. Often Beatrice would knit and, if Greta were reading, she'd listen to a book being read on her phone, one earbud inserted, in case Greta spoke to her. It was comfortable and the rain beating on the window made it feel especially cozy tonight.

"What do you think of Bertie Frankel, Beatrice?"

"I think he's a nice man. He certainly likes coming to visit you."

"Well, he's been coming to visit me for a very long time, in one role or another. We've been friends since high school."

"Just friends? Sometimes I think he seems like he's sweet on you."

Greta colored slightly. "Oh, there was a time when that was probably true, but our timing was always terrible." Greta picked up her book. "Life is full of missed opportunities, isn't it?"

Beatrice quietly knitted and listened to her audio book. She was working on a sweet unicorn hat for one of the Spencer girls, her girls, as she thought of them. She missed them, and their mother had capitulated and allowed her to visit on their new nanny's day off. Of course, that meant that their mom didn't have to pay anyone to watch them that day, so it worked out for everyone, although Mrs. Spencer acted like she was doing Beatrice a huge favor.

Greta had been quiet for some time and Bea though she was asleep when she spoke again. "When I was married to my first husband, Bertie was single. He hung out with our group and brought lots of pretty girls to the house. Then Harold was killed just after Bertie and Annabelle were married. By the time Annabelle divorced Bertie, I was already married to Gregory. It just never worked out."

Beatrice didn't know what to say to that, and it didn't really seem like Greta was talking to her as much as just thinking it through.

A few minutes later Greta had set her book aside and her even breathing told Bea that the medications had lulled her into a comfortable sleep.

Bea got up and put the book aside, made sure the water jug was full, and changed the light to dim so that the older woman wouldn't awaken in the night and be afraid. Just like her little Spencer girls and their unicorn night light.

Tomorrow would be a long and difficult day for both of them. They would need to wake early for their trip to the University of San Francisco Medical Center for Greta's checkup. In many ways it was as tedious and complex as preparing children for an outing. Greta hated to leave the house without feeling like she looked her best. The process of showering and selecting the right outfit, putting on makeup, and arranging one of her wigs into a flattering style tired her so much that she was more ready for a nap than an outing by the time they were done.

The packing for the outing would include a change of clothes, wipes, medications, snacks, everything that Beatrice had needed to take for the little ones when she worked as a nanny.

Getting Greta to the car and into it, and the walker and wheelchair, neither of which she wanted to use, into the trunk needed to be done patiently and caringly to not get her upset.

Beatrice usually drove Greta's car and they had finally worked out a process of stopping at the unloading zone outside the center where Beatrice would unload and set up the wheelchair, help Greta into it, and push her into the lobby, leaving her and her extensive paraphernalia in a convenient spot to wait while she found parking.

CHAPTER SIX

That Tuesday there were several appointments lined up back-to-back. First the lab, then the clinic, then to the pharmacy, and finally reversing the process for getting her back home and up to her bedroom. By then both of them would be exhausted.

Since Greta had been enrolled in a clinical trial being run at the cancer center the visits happened more often and she had more labs and scans than she'd been having before. Beatrice had not been in favor of Greta's joining the study. She'd read the protocols and the informed consent and it seemed to her that these companies just dangled hope in front of terminally ill patients when all the FDA-approved treatments had failed.

Beatrice supposed that someone had to be in the trials but it didn't seem right to her to take battered sick people and use them as experimental animals. Maybe someone else down the road would benefit, but it probably would not be Greta.

The one good thing about the trial was that Greta did love the extra attention, and maybe it did make her feel better to think she was doing something positive. She certainly liked her visits with the study coordinator, Sandeep Sheik, Sandy as she called him, had been a physician trained in India, but when he came to the United States the requirements for certification were a huge hurdle. For now, he had taken a position working as a coordinator handling clinical trials at the cancer center.

Perhaps, if Sandeep had struggled mightily for his degree and not been brought up in such an entitled manner, he'd have viewed his temporary setback in a better light. It wasn't impossible to become credentialed in the U.S., but it rankled that he felt he'd already done the work. In fact, he felt he was smarter and better than most of the doctors he worked for.

When he'd lived at home his mother had regularly left manila envelopes with the résumés of potential wives on his bedside table for his consideration. In the U.S. he hadn't really dated much. He wasn't sure how to carry it off, to be honest. Why should he make the effort to be charming and appeal to the women he met? They should be trying to charm him.

Sharing an apartment with a couple of medical students who made an annoying habit of requiring him to clean up his own messes and provide his own food had not been what he'd expected either. Of course, he hadn't had to settle down in as expensive an area as San Francisco, but he couldn't picture himself in the Midwest or Southern United States.

The position he had taken working as a study coordinator on clinical trials had given him hope that he could get himself a decent job working for one of the biotech or medical device companies. Maybe he wouldn't have to redo his residency, after all.

While the doctors and nurses were no fonder of him than he was of them, the lady patients in his trials loved him. He knew he was good-looking and could be pleasant when he wanted to; when he thought there might be something in it for him. Greta Gardner, for example. She was, of course, much older than he, and her illness had taken quite a toll, but he could tell she adored him and showed great sympathy toward the sad situation he found himself in. He thought, if she had more time he could convince her to have him move into her Presidio Heights home, rent-free. And she was already making noises about altering her trust to leave him money to help him complete his studies here, maybe get his practice started, or whatever he could convince her he needed. It was too bad that one of the inclusion criteria for the study she was enrolled in required a life expectancy of twelve weeks. At least, in her case, she had already lasted longer than that and seemed to be determined to hang in as long as she could.

Some of the other women patients— alone, sad, and afraid— had only managed to provide him with a few gifts and a couple of bequests before their cancers got the best of them. One of them had gifted him a very nice automobile though he'd had to sell it since there was limited parking near his home. If he lived on Walnut Street he'd have access to a garage. He'd wandered past Greta's house a couple of times and could imagine himself in that neighborhood, although he didn't know what the ultra-white neighbors would think. She also had a nice car that he could get access to. He had seen her coming to the cancer center with her servant driving. Though, of course he knew better than to refer to Beatrice as a servant. What was wrong with using that word anyway? When he had referred to her that way Greta had been quick to correct him. He should say "companion" or "staff," he was told.

Today, when he went to the waiting room he found Greta sitting in one of the chairs with Beatrice beside her. He thought it was incredibly vain that Greta insisted on moving from the wheelchair stowed in the corner so that she was sitting in a regular chair and could walk, unaided, into his office, although he was careful to support her by holding her elbow for the short journey.

Greta had slumped down in her chair until she saw Sandy enter the room and she perked up a bit. She so looked forward to these visits. It was quite the ego boost to have half an hour or more of exclusive attention from a young, handsome man.

"Ah, good morning Ms. Gardner, how is my favorite patient today?" Sandy strode across the waiting room and took Greta's hand to help her from her seat.

"Much better since I get to see you. And, please, you must call me Greta. Ms. Gardner was my mother."

Sandeep smiled broadly. "You flatter me, Greta." As Greta struggled to her feet, Beatrice stood as well. Sandeep waved his free hand at her dismissively. "I can take her from here, there's no need for you to accompany us."

Beatrice sat back down and cast the man a stony look.

The young man supported Greta with his hand on her arm and walked her through the doors to the clinic area as Beatrice pulled her latest knitting project from her bag.

It was not a long walk to the examination room and he noted that Greta seemed less winded and a little stronger than she had on earlier visits.

He was not performing much of an examination today, mostly vital signs. The real data would come from the scheduled labs and scans. "It looks like you have gained a couple of pounds since your last visit."

"Really, Sandy, don't you know you should never comment on a lady's weight?" Greta's cheeks had turned a bit pink.

"Well, in your case it is definitely a good thing."

Sandeep checked her pulse and blood pressure and listened to her heart. For most patients this was something a medical assistant could do, but he liked to have time for private conversations with some of his study subjects. When he was done he sat companionably in the side chair. "Now is when you need to tell me about any adverse events or reactions you have experienced since your last visit."

Greta thought for a moment. "There really aren't any to speak of. Of course, I still feel like holy hell most of the time, but no worse than before, and I think a bit better."

"Then tell me about your positive events. There's no place to put those on the case report forms, but I am still very interested to hear them."

"First, I need to remember to tell you that I am meeting with my attorney next week to make sure that your foundation gets the funding it needs when I am gone."

"That is great to hear, but, at the rate you are going, I will be old and gray before that happens."

Only Greta laughed.

CHAPTER SEVEN

Annabelle Leigh, what a ridiculous name. She wished her mother hadn't been such a fan of Edgar Allan Poe. Mom had claimed that she picked the name because she thought it melodious, but Annabelle had been haunted by the specter of the macabre poet her entire life.

She sat in her car in the rainy mist. Some cars parked on the street any length of time in this neighborhood would have caused suspicion, but a new Tesla was always a welcome guest.

Annabelle had just returned from living in Florida for several years, and the cold, gray day had her rethinking her decision. Still, Greta was here in San Francisco, and more importantly, so was Bertie. She'd been doing some snooping around, not that difficult in her old circle here. She'd been able to keep a pretty low profile even while gathering the information she needed to proceed with her plan. Now that her very wealthy, older, and childless husband had died, it was very good news to her that Bertie had fallen on, if not hard times, at least tentative times. She'd had lunch with Carlton Drummond, Bertie's financial adviser, luring him in by dangling her newly inherited fortune in front of his nose. She snorted; he was so transparent. It had been pretty damned easy to get the lowdown on Bertie's investments while securing the promise to not mention he'd seen her to their mutual acquaintances. If this all worked out she wouldn't care if he managed her and Bertie's money together. She just wanted to be Annabelle Frankel again. She'd also been able to determine through other friends that Greta was ill. Not just ill, but dying, so her greatest rival would soon be out of the picture, for good.

In school she and Greta had been friends, close friends. Close enough that Greta knew that Annabelle loved funny little Bertie Frankel more than anything else. Greta didn't mind because she didn't really want him, but she was intrigued by her newly realized ability to get and keep his attention, no matter how it affected her dear friend. After all, it wasn't like she was seriously interested herself. It wasn't really her fault that Bertie was so besotted with her. Greta had never told anyone how Annabelle felt about Bertie. Not from any loyalty, but because it allowed her to continue to manipulate them both.

Once Greta had married her first husband, Harold, the way was clear for Annabelle. Greta's outrageous flirting with Bertie was laughed off by everyone around them, even after Bertie and Annabelle were married. And then, when that moron Harold died in that stupid motorcycle accident, there was Greta leaning on her two very best friends for comfort.

Annabelle had been ecstatic in her marriage. She'd hoped for children; she'd invited Greta to be her matron of honor. She'd done everything she could to be a good wife to Bertie and he had been happy enough. Annabelle was pretty, and socially acceptable. She was capable in a way that neither Bertie, nor Greta, would ever be. Everything worked like clockwork. They bought the right house in the best neighborhood. They had the nicest dinner parties, they belonged to the best clubs, and went on the best vacations with their compatriots at the Bohemian Club. Bertie didn't really have to worry about anything, he was well taken care of. But, when poor, sad, widowed Greta came around, things went south pretty quickly.

At first Annabelle was sympathetic. She'd have been devastated if anything had happened to Bertie, so she included Greta in all her plans. She began to see Bertie drawing away from her, taking Greta's side when they argued about how demanding she was getting, ranting and raving whenever Greta seemed to have a new man. Of course, at the time, Annabelle had not known how much of Bertie's time was taken up with lunches, dinners, and outings with Greta. When she did find out, she demanded that Bertie cease and desist. He wouldn't and he couldn't though they struggled with it for several months, and, by the time that Annabelle had had enough and obtained a divorce Greta had run off and married her second husband, Gregory, and Bertie was left in the lurch. At first Annabelle was elated. Now that Greta was off the market, she could work on getting Bertie back home.

Fortunately, she had enough self-respect to throw in the towel after several months of comforting Bertie in his mourning. She had moved to New York, met someone else, married, and moved to Florida. But now, her husband was dead. He had been good to her and a nice man, but he was gone and his significant fortune was hers. She had come back for Bertie but had not counted on the additional pleasure of watching Greta die a lingering death. This time she was prepared to console poor Bertie while he got over his loss. This time, she had all the time and patience in the world.

The downstairs lights had been on for some time when the upstairs front bedroom light went on. When they were children that had been Greta's parents' bedroom, but Annabelle reasoned that Greta had moved into the primary suite by now. She would give Greta a little time to pull herself together before she made her appearance at the front door. The heavy scent of the bouquet of stargazer lilies filled the warm car and she occupied herself by playing on her phone. She had hit the flower market on Brannan Street early and then swung past the Estelle Pâtisserie to buy a box of fresh pastries. You didn't want to just drop into someone's life without bringing gifts.

Annabelle flipped down the visor to take another look at herself in the mirror.

She was looking good. She could afford the best of the best and the Botox and lip plumping had been seamless and artful. The years spent under the sun in Florida had given her a glow, maybe a little enhanced by a spray tan, and her hair was streaked golden by both the sun and a skillful beautician.

She pulled the hood of her London Fog up over her head. Armed with the flowers and the pink bakery box she dashed across the street and up the steps.

The bell was answered by a tall woman dressed in bright colors. Annabelle had heard that Greta had a hired companion staying with her and was prepared to be gracious to the help. She herself had never been able to keep household staff for long. She was too cheap to pay really well and demanded a level of service and acquiescence beyond the scope of the people she'd hired.

Well, she didn't need staff for the little place she had rented for now. Someone came in and tidied up a couple of times a week, and with the food delivery services that abounded in the city she could get whatever she wanted to eat, whenever she wanted it.

"Good morning, ma'am. May I help you?"

"Oh, yes. I'm Annabelle, an old friend of Ms. Gardner. I was hoping to catch her at home and up to receiving visitors."

"Please come in out of the weather." The tall woman stepped back from the door the beads of her braids clattering together softly. "Let me take your coat."

"Thank you so much. Do you think Greta is awake?"

"Oh, yes ma'am. She's up and had her tea and toast." Beatrice took the damp coat from the woman and hung it to dry on the hall tree. "Let me run up and let her know that you are here. What did you say your name is again?"

"Annabelle Leigh. It's been a long time, but I'm sure she'll remember me."

When Beatrice had disappeared up the stairs Annabelle hung her purse next to the coat and placed the bakery box and flowers on the table. She checked herself out in the mirror and took a moment to fluff her hair.

It wasn't very often that Greta's friends just dropped in. Usually, they came when invited for tea or cocktails, or called before coming.

Beatrice knocked lightly on the bedroom door.

"Yes, Beatrice. What is it?" Greta had not slept well and was hoping to cuddle back down for a nap.

"Sorry to disturb you, Greta, but you have a guest. Annabelle Leigh?"

Greta sat bolt upright in her bed. "Annabelle Leigh is here? In San Francisco? Downstairs?"

"Yes, ma'am. She just showed up with a pastry box and a bouquet of flowers. Should I show her up?"

"No…yes, wait a minute. I haven't seen Annabelle in years. Help me straighten up and get me my bed jacket."

After a flurry of activity, with her wig firmly placed, her bed jacket on, a swipe of pink lipstick, and the various books, magazines, tissues, and throat lozenge wrappers swept out of sight Greta was ready.

"Okay, now you can show her up." Greta heaved a huge sigh of relief as Beatrice headed downstairs. What was Annabelle doing here? It's not like they had kept in touch after that ugly scene at Greta's wedding to Gregory. Still, it would be lovely to see her again.

CHAPTER EIGHT

At the bottom of the stairs Annabelle waited patiently. She had sidled to each of the doors that led into the entry hall and scoped out the status of the house. Of course, it had been remodeled during the time Greta and Gregory had lived there, but it had not been updated in a while. The colors were old and the house was showing its age, as she assumed Greta was, as well. She could already feel a frisson of excitement thinking about what she would do if, or when, she got her hands on the house. She and Greta had always had very different tastes, except in men.

She really longed to wander through the place, both to check all the rooms, and to remember the good times here when they had grown up together. She wouldn't have been surprised to find their hidey-hole, where they had stashed cigarettes, joints, secret notes, and condoms, still under the stairs in the storage area. It probably still concealed some very dry marijuana crumbles and other contraband. Did condoms go bad, over time?

She heard Beatrice close the door to the bedroom and hurriedly stepped back into the center of the entry.

"Ms. Leigh, Ms. Gardner would be so happy if you would go on up. It's the first door on the right. Let me put the flowers in a vase and bring up some tea, or would you prefer coffee?"

"Tea would be lovely. The box has some of Greta's favorite pastries from the little shop we used to go to."

Beatrice picked the flowers and pastry box off the table and hurried off toward the kitchen. Annabelle paused for a moment looking up the stairs before she proceeded up. She paused once more outside the bedroom door before knocking lightly.

"Come in, come in, Annabelle."

Entering the room Annabelle couldn't help but be taken aback by how illness had ravaged Greta. She looked so frail that, for a brief second, Annabelle wished they were still friends and that she could sweep her up in her arms and make things better. Greta looked so like the young woman Annabelle had comforted after her botched abortion at seventeen. The one that kept her from ever having the children she'd always wanted.

Greta spoke first. "Annabelle, Annabelle, it is so amazing to see you. You look wonderful, just like always." In fact, Annabelle looked better than Greta ever remembered her looking. As a youngster Annabelle had been careless of her looks and tended to fade into the background, although she had been the smarter of the two of them. She had clung to her intelligence with a mighty grip, often putting their friends off with her need to display her knowledge and show off her academic achievements. Now she looked positively bursting with health, the one real thing that she had that Greta did not. Her style was understated except that everything about her subtly whispered money.

"Greta, you are looking great. I was so sorry to hear that you've been ill."

"You are a terrible liar, Annabelle, about my looks, of course."

They both laughed self-consciously.

"Sit down, sit down." Greta motioned to the chair next to the bed." Back in the day she'd have patted the bed next to her, but that was a bit too intimate for this encounter. "Is Beatrice getting us some tea?"

"Yes, I believe she is."

"It really is so lovely to see you. I had no idea you were here from

Florida. Will you be here long?"

"I hope so. I've sold the estate in Florida and moved to a little rental not too far from here. When everything settles out from the trust and insurance and all I'll be buying something here. Maybe not right in San Francisco, but close by."

"I was so sorry to hear that your husband had passed, Annie. Had he been ill for long?"

"Well, he was much older than I am, so I suppose it wasn't a great surprise. He was very active right up until the end. Died right there on the eleventh hole at Mar-a-Lago, of course they kept that part quiet. Not really good for business, you know."

"Well…that's too bad." What else could Greta say?

The conversation languished for several seconds until Annabelle picked up the opened book on the bedside table. "I see you still love trashy romances."

"Yes, you know me. I used to get four of them mailed to me in a plain brown wrapper from Harlequin so Mummy wouldn't know what trash I was reading."

"Do you remember that scandalous book we both read when we were younger, *The Passion Flower Hotel*?"

"Oh, my God, yes! I thought she was going to have a heart attack when she found it under my bed." The mention of a heart attack, considering Annabelle's husband's recent demise, again stopped the conversation.

Greta was grateful when Beatrice returned to the bedroom wielding a giant bouquet of Stargazer lilies. They were truly beautiful, and Annabelle must have forgotten how allergic Greta was to them.

As Beatrice moved to put them next to the bed Greta waved her away. "Put them over there, on the far table by the window."

"I'll be right back up with some tea and the lovely pastries Ms. Leigh brought."

"That is such a nice gesture, Annabelle. Flowers and sweeties."

"I couldn't resist. I got them at that little place where we used to buy them after school. I was so excited to see that it was still open after all these decades."

"Well, it's very sweet of you. I didn't even know you were in town." Greta hesitated. "Of course, I don't usually get kept up to date on the latest news." She almost mentioned that her best source of gossip was Bertie, who she remembered was Annabelle's ex-husband and that, unfortunately, Annabelle blamed her for the divorce. Instead, she said, "I am mostly dependent on visits from old friends and that trashy and irresistible blog, *SFUndertheRug.com*. I don't know where they come up with all that stuff, but it is entertaining."

"I don't know anything about the blog, but not many people are aware that I'm here. Even fewer know that I am moving back to the city."

Greta was surprised that Annabelle was moving back to San Francisco. She'd been mightily angry with all of their circle when she'd moved away, especially with Greta and Bertie.

Downstairs, Beatrice had put on the kettle and set up the tea tray. While she waited for the tea to steep she sent a quick text to Kestrel: *Annabelle Leigh visiting Greta. Know anything?* Beatrice counted herself among Kestrel's many informants, although she tried to not be too judgmental about the shenanigans she witnessed among the wealthy. Beatrice knew that Kestrel would be interested to know that Annabelle Leigh was back in town. Kestrel hadn't been doing her blog when the Greta/Bertie/Annabelle brouhaha had erupted but they had both heard tales of it during their time in San Francisco.

As she was removing the tea ball from the pot her phone buzzed back. *Hell, yeah. Old friends who became old enemies. Only know the rumors. See what you can find out.*

There didn't seem to be much tension in the room when Beatrice returned bearing refreshments. The two ladies were chatting away about old friends and schoolgirl days. Beatrice moved around the room unobtrusively picking up stray items and generally looking busy while she kept her ears open for any tidbits of information. There wasn't much to learn, as all of the times they discussed were long gone, but she did glean the fact that Annabelle considered herself here to stay. She no doubt would get a better understanding of how Greta felt about that when her visitor was gone.

Greta had begun to tire, and her head ached from the being in the vicinity of the lilies. How could Annabelle have forgotten how allergic she was? One time she had to leave a dinner party early when she'd gotten so sick she couldn't stay around the flowers a moment longer. Bertie had left Annabelle to get a ride home for herself while he escorted Greta to her house.

Annabelle rose from her chair. "I can see you are getting tired, dear. I am going to leave and let you get some rest, but I'll be back to visit soon."

Greta didn't seem to feel the faint vibe of malice that Beatrice detected. But maybe that was just because Beatrice had not taken an instant liking to Annabelle. She thought she was a pretty good judge of people at first sight, and her first sense of Annabelle was a touch of distrust.

At the bottom of the stairs Annabelle turned. "Do you think I could use the powder room before I head out?"

"Certainly, ma'am. It's just down the hallway."

"No need to show me, I know this house like the back of my hand."

In the powder room, Annabelle quickly peed, taking a moment to think about how this tiny room could be upgraded. She'd need one of those Japanese bidet toilets, for sure. She'd had them installed in all five bathrooms in her Florida home, and even the one in the pool house.

The rain had slackened a bit when she returned to her car, and she sat there for a few more minutes assessing the landscaping around the Walnut Street address. Those horrendous rhododendrons would have to go, and the ivy on the wall. She eventually drove away, unaware that Beatrice had stood at the upstairs window watching her dally in front of the house.

Greta was already dozing in the bed when Beatrice took the vase of lilies down the stairs. She'd take them to her room at the back of the house, where they wouldn't bother Greta.

CHAPTER NINE

Sandeep, or Sandy as he preferred, had not slept well. The clinical research associate from the drug company running one of his trials would be on-site for the rest of the week and he'd not had time to keep up the data collection the way they wanted. The woman had notified him that she'd checked the status online and he would need to bring things up to date while she was there. Didn't she understand that he was busy? There really should be someone who did this data entry work.

He got into the clinic early and attacked the stack of patient files waiting on his desk. He was one of the most successful enrollers for the trial, and keeping up with all the visits was taking up all his time without having to spend hours inputting data into the sponsor's database. On top of that burden, the woman would be checking his work, item by item, asking a lot of questions, and expecting immediate corrections to any problems she found.

There was a lot of pressure in getting everything entered for this trial in a timely manner. The pharmaceutical company wanted to do an interim analysis of all the data so they could make some decisions. It looked like they might be getting some good results, but you couldn't really tell until the blind was broken and the data analyzed.

It seemed to him that some of his patients were doing well. Their cancers were taking longer to progress than was usual. Of course, he couldn't tell what that really meant since it was a randomized trial. Some of the patients received a combination of the experimental drug with an FDA-approved therapy and some received the approved drug and a placebo. The experimental drug and placebo were packaged identically and identified with randomly assigned numbers.

Sadly, one of his subjects seemed to be doing really well. She'd been in the week before for a scheduled follow-up and he'd just gotten the results of her scans and lab work. The bloody woman was flourishing. The scans showed not just no progression, but even possible improvement of her tumors. Of course, the doctors and the drug company would be elated, but then, they weren't waiting for her to die to receive a promised bequest in her will.

He'd had to get pretty cagey about how these things were done. It wouldn't be ethical for him to be getting inheritances from his patients, but, if you set it up right, nobody would ever know.

First he'd set up a research non-profit that showed no connection to him personally, then he'd ingratiated himself with the lonely, pitiful, older women enrolled in the trial.

He'd been careful, too. The women that he took extra effort to impress were the ones who didn't have close family, were unmarried, and ate up the flattery and charm he poured over them. And, most importantly, they had money and property. Having a close informant in the UCSF Finance Department had been invaluable, but that had its own pitfalls. There was a price to pay for everything.

Nobody would notice or care if his little organization received part of their estates. Nobody would even notice or ever ask where the money went, and, oddly, the women themselves never pursued asking about what his foundation accomplished. He'd tried to manage the funds with great care. He needed it to last to support his plans, but the bank account had become low and he'd found himself calculating how long he'd have to wait to collect on some of them.

Greta Gardner had been his ace in the hole. Her cancer had been advanced metastatic when she'd been recruited into the study and she barely met the Inclusion/Exclusion Criteria. In fact, he'd had to fudge a bit on the criterion of "a life expectancy of twelve weeks."

Now, months into the trial, she was thriving. He'd sat in on the panel meeting of doctors reviewing the cases and had tried to determine how long they thought she might live. The standard six to twelve months they were giving her if things stayed the same was great news for her, but not so much for him.

He'd be meeting her to give her the results of her tests later this week. As he lay awake last night it had occurred to him that he might go to her home to personally give her the results. Of course, that wasn't the standard of care, but he was curious to see her home and find out her living circumstances. She'd always come for her visits accompanied by a companion, but Sandy didn't know how that worked. Did the woman live with her, or was there someone else in the house?

Once he'd gotten the data monitor woman settled in the coldest, most cramped section of the office with her stack of patient files, logged her into the cancer center computers, and helped her dodge her way through getting connected to the electronic data capture (EDC) system for her company, he retired to his desk and closed the door. He pulled out his cell phone and scrolled through the numbers of his patients and connections. Sandy didn't really have friends. The people he felt it appropriate to be friends with, the doctors at the hospital, did not give him the time of day, and he felt the rest of the staff were beneath him. Only his contact in the finance department was of any value to him.

Damn, the phone went directly to voicemail. He hung up and gave some thought to what kind of message he wanted to leave. He wanted her to call him back right away, but he didn't want to leave any message that he might come to her house. Once he'd thought it through, he called back, got her voicemail again, and left the message that he wanted to convey her recent test results and leaving his cell number. He wanted to make sure she would be alone when he went to the house, not that it mattered what her companion thought, but it wasn't really kosher for him to go there. Much better if only he and Greta knew he had come. She'd be flattered to have a secret to share with him.

CHAPTER TEN

Bertie was happy to see that Greta had sent him a text until he read it. Holy shit, Annabelle was moving back to San Francisco. His first feeling was a bit of guilt over the way he had treated his ex-wife. He'd been happy to hear that she'd married again, and he'd heard married well, as defined by a lot of money. She'd been living in Florida the last time he'd heard about her— not from her, she'd sworn she'd never speak to him again when they got divorced and, up until now, she'd kept her word.

He texted back, quickly, *The husband?*

The answer came almost instantly, *Dead.*

Texting back and forth like this was not giving him the info he needed but he was stuck in this meeting with Carlton and his banker. It took a half hour for him to get a break and go someplace private to make the call. It went directly to voicemail, so she was probably taking a nap. If he could ever get out of this interminable meeting he could swing by her house in the early evening. He really needed to get Beatrice's personal cell phone. It would be easy to give her a call and dig up whatever information she could give. Not that she was particularly open with him. He suspected she thought he was an arrogant shit, which he had to admit, he probably was. He'd just never felt it was necessary to be all chummy with the help. The closest he needed to get was grudgingly handing over the salary that they demanded.

Bertie had gotten out of the meeting by promising to sit down and go through the budget documents they had prepared and consider making some changes to his lifestyle. He supposed that they were right when they said that; considering the reversal of his fortunes the past couple of years, he could probably make some cuts to the luxuries of his life. Still, it rankled. Bertie was terrible with money. He'd never been good about it, but he'd never had to be "good" before. Many of the perks of his life were just things he'd grown up having and, until now, had never had to consider the cost of them: symphony tickets, opera tickets, PU Club membership and the required monthly expenditures, and Bohemian Club membership.

Carl and the banker had been careful to assure him that he wasn't broke. If he invested more of his funds appropriately and cut down on cash expenditures, his fortune would last the rest of his life. The problem was, he just didn't want to cut back on any of those things and he found it insulting and embarrassing to even have to discuss money with other people. It was just so gauche to talk about money, especially the lack of it.

Dropping hints about how much something cost was an entirely different matter. What was the point of buying something expensive if nobody knew what it cost? He was blissfully unaware of his reputation for being far too revealing about what he spent on things. He was a nice man, and a longtime friend, so most people ignored his faux pas, only rolling their eyes at one another when he launched into the financial details of his latest purchase or vacation.

He'd listened carefully while Carlton expounded on his need to economize and the rabbity banker nodded in agreement, but they didn't know what he knew. That Greta Gardner, whose illness everyone agreed was so sad, had pretty much promised that some of her estate would be coming to him when she passed, which it appeared might be very soon. His being her main heir would inevitably engender a fair amount of gossip and speculation, even if most of it was false. She hadn't been his secret lover, but she appreciated that he had supported her their whole lives, even to the point of letting his devotion contribute to the destruction of his only marriage. He provided the kind of flattery, service, and caring that was hard to come by, even though, as she reasoned, he had nothing to gain from her since he had his own fortune. Certainly, he had never shared his changed circumstance with her. Annabelle had called it "slavish devotion," but she didn't really understand the role Greta had in his life. He wasn't sure he understood either, but since they were children together, when Greta had first begun to include him in her charmed circle of friends, she'd given him validation of his worthiness to be there. With her supporting him he'd become a more confident person. He'd never thought he could really have her in the way some people thought of it, but even the fact that other people thought he was worthy of that attention, gave him great satisfaction.

Now, his devotion was going to be rewarded in the way that would be most useful to him. She didn't know, but he knew, that her money would allow him to maintain his lifestyle and the confidence that she had helped build.

CHAPTER ELEVEN

When Greta woke, she lay very still for a while. It was not dark yet and the gray of the San Francisco afternoon seeped into her unlit room. She felt cozy and quite comfortable and did not even want to raise her arm to look at her watch. Someone had told her that it was very old-fashioned to wear a watch. All the young people used their phones to tell time. Still, she'd paid a lot of money for her timepiece, back when it was the in-thing to own, and she didn't like carrying her phone with her everywhere she went. That required pockets in everything, and a designer had told her once that pockets spoil the line of your clothes. Although, considering that she usually wore only the equivalent of designer sweatsuits anymore, it probably didn't matter. She'd seen a kind of watch that was a phone sort of thing, but it was clunky and ugly, probably right in style these days.

For a few minutes she just lay there, refreshed from her nap, and thought about how good she was really feeling. Her initial cancer diagnosis had thrown her for a loop, and she had taken full advantage of her invalid state. But soon, even she had grown tired of the main topic of conversation being her health and her treatment. Lately she had been feeling much better and she was beginning to think that her usual slothful ways were getting boring.

To tell the truth, she probably didn't even need Beatrice full-time anymore, but she did so enjoy being waited upon.

Sitting up, she finally looked at her watch. Four o'clock, just about what she thought. She noticed the pastries still sitting on the tea tray across the room and realized she was hungry.

Getting up she pulled her silky robe around her. It had gotten quite large, or rather she had gotten quite small—the only advantage to her illness being that her weight dropped easily and effortlessly. In fact, it was much more of an effort to eat. Still, the past few days she had eaten more than her usual few bites and right now she was solely focused on the lovely macarons that Annabelle had brought. The teapot was still full but gone cold. She considered whether to ring for Beatrice. No, she was quite enjoying just being on her own. She poured some of the tea into her cup and placed several of the dainty cookies on a small plate. She would sit by the window and watch the world go by instead of getting back in bed. She was grateful that she'd upgraded the heating system and the room was quite warm, although it looked very dismal outside.

Before she sat down she retrieved her cell phone from the bedside charger. She might not want to carry it with her everywhere she went, but she loved having it available when she wanted it. What a wonder the little thing was. Settled at last she fired up the iPhone and saw that she had gotten a couple of calls. She preferred texts. It was like a little tennis match lobbing and slamming *bon mots* back and forth. It wasn't nearly as much fun to talk to someone about whatever mundane things had been going on in their lives.

The first message was from Bertie. He wanted to come by. She was sure he did since her little bombshell about Annabelle showing up. The second message was from Sandy at the cancer center. He had her results. That didn't sound nearly as interesting so she pushed the magic little button on the phone and called Bertie back.

"Hello, Greta. Thanks for calling back. I hope I didn't disturb your nap."

"Nothing could have disturbed my nap, Bertie. I was dead to the world."

"Good, that's good. Hope you're feeling better. Now, tell me about Annabelle. How did you hear she's back?"

"She came to the house to see me."

"She…she came to your house?"

"Yes, this morning, she came to the house bearing gifts. You know what they say about Greeks bearing gifts."

"Do you know how long she'll be here? I hadn't heard a peep from anyone that they've heard from her."

"She's not just visiting. She's here to stay, moving back here."

"Did she say what happened to her husband?"

"Yes, dropped dead on the golf course. She sold the estate in Florida, gathered up his insurance money, and she is going to buy something here. I think she's been keeping it hush-hush, for now."

"Wow, that is unexpected. I wonder why she came back here. How is she?" Bertie seemed to realize that it might be expected that he ask about the health of his recently widowed ex-wife.

"Actually, she looks great, and seems well. She's definitely had some work done, I'd say, and her tan is fabulous."

"Well, that's good news, I guess. I really don't know what to think, I'm so gobsmacked."

"It was a surprise, all right. Did your message say you were thinking of coming by later?"

Bertie was rethinking the necessity of going to Greta's house on this wintry evening. It would be so much easier to just order some food delivered from his favorite Italian restaurant down the street and open a bottle of wine. He had fallen into the habit of spending his evenings binge-watching Netflix when he didn't have dinner plans someplace. When he was younger he often felt the need of constant company but these days he'd just as soon stay home. Besides, he needed to give some thought to Annabelle's return. What it meant, what it would affect, and most importantly, how it might affect him. Annabelle had always been charming and Annabelle with a very large fortune was even more alluring. He wondered idly if he'd completely spoiled his chances with her. "I was hoping to come over and see you, but I think I'm coming down with a cold and don't want to expose you. Maybe I should wait a couple of days." He coughed unconvincingly into the phone.

"Sure, Bertie, that would be fine. But be sure to let me know before you come. I am feeling so great these days I might be out."

"Okay, dear, see you soon." He coughed again. What did she mean about feeling so great? Too much to think about.

Greta popped the last of the macarons into her mouth and smiled at the empty plate. My, my, her appetite was definitely improving.

She checked her watch to confirm that it was still before five p.m. to make sure she'd be able to catch Sandy before he left the cancer center. Yep, she still had a few minutes and he was her next call.

The call went through quickly and rang just twice before Sandy picked up his phone, "Sandeep Sheik, UCSF Cancer Center."

"Hello, Sandy, it's me, Ms. Gardner, returning your call."

"Ah yes, Ms. Gardner. So good to hear from you." Sandy stepped across his small office to close the door. "I was just calling to give you an update on your most recent follow-up visit. Is this a good time?"

"It is a great time, especially if it is good news."

"Well, actually it is pretty good news, but I would really like to give it to you in person."

"You mean I need to come back into the center?"

Sandy laughed. "No, no, I meant I might have an opportunity to come by your place and talk to you about what is going on. I wondered when would be good for you."

"Well, except when I have doctor's appointments I am pretty much always home. So, almost anytime is good, I guess." Greta laughed, as well. It was kind of exciting that Sandy might want to come by and see her.

"It isn't really a problem, but I am not sure of the propriety of going to your home. Does your companion who brings you for visits live there with you?"

"Yes, Beatrice has a room here and she's usually around unless she goes shopping or running errands. Of course, she has days off, but she is not much of a social butterfly. Wait, I know, she's going to be away on Saturday, spending time with some old friends. But that breaks into your weekend, so that wouldn't work."

"No, in fact that is perfect. I have a clinical monitor here this week reviewing all the data from the study you are on, so it would be hard to get away. In fact, I will probably be here late tonight getting things finished for her. Saturday would be great. When would be a good time?"

"I'll have to get back to you, I'm not sure when she is going out on Saturday. Can I call and leave you a message tomorrow?"

"Sure, that would be fine. I think you will be really encouraged by your progress."

"I'll call and leave you a message tomorrow, Sandy. I look forward to seeing you."

When she'd gotten off the phone Greta was kind of excited to be having company, male company, even if he was way too young for her. She was surprised she even felt good enough to think of him as male.

Beatrice came quietly upstairs and tapped on the door, not wanting to wake Greta if she was still sleeping.

"Come in."

Beatrice was surprised to see Greta sitting at the window next to an empty cookie plate. There was a bit of pink in her cheeks and she seemed unusually animated. "I hope you had a good nap. You certainly look rested."

"Yes, I did and I feel fine tonight. How was your afternoon?"

"It was very nice. I've been working on my little gifts I've been knitting for my girls and I am almost finished."

Greta had gotten used to Beatrice referring to her former nanny charges as "her girls." She had been with the Spencer family most of the twins' young lives but fell away as a victim of a particularly nasty divorce. Greta was glad that Sharon Spencer, not one of her favorite people, let Beatrice stay in touch with them. "Oh yes, I meant to ask you, what time do you think you'll be leaving on Saturday?"

"I was planning to leave about nine in the morning so that we have the whole day, but I can change those plans if you need something."

"No, not at all, I was just wondering."

Beatrice was relieved as she'd made elaborate plans to entertain Lisbeth and Lucy. She was quite excited about them herself. "So, I've got a nice dinner going for you, are you hungry?"

Greta glanced guiltily at the empty plate beside her and realized she was still hungry. "Yes, actually I am quite ready for dinner. But, before that, you know what I would love? A hot soak in the tub and some wine. Could you run the bath for me and get me a glass of wine? I am thinking I might even want to come downstairs for dinner tonight."

Beatrice smiled broadly. "Yes, ma'am. I can run you a bath. I'll put in your favorite scent and light some candles. What do you think, rose or lavender?"

"I think lavender, it always gives me a lift."

Beatrice immediately started the bath in the huge, jetted tub in the master bathroom. She tested the water carefully and lit some of the multiple candles that sat around the tub. She also turned on the radiant heater in the ceiling to warm the room and then headed out to get the wine. "Red wine or white, Greta?"

"I think something bubbly to go with the bath."

When Beatrice returned with the wine and a couple of luxuriously fluffy fresh towels Greta had slipped out of her lounge clothes and robe and into the warmly scented, sudsy water. Beatrice turned on the bath jets.

"I'll go set the table and get dinner finished. Is the kitchen table all right?

"Yes, the kitchen is perfect. Thank you Beatrice. Could you light the incense in the lamp, please?"

Greta watched as Beatrice placed a fresh cone of incense into the cheap brass lamp she'd had for so many years. She had bought it on a whim at the import store when she was a young girl and had used it ever since. She'd always joked with people that it was her magic lamp that could transport her to wherever she wanted to go. It had become a long-standing custom to light it when she bathed.

It took about twenty minutes for Beatrice to set the table for two and dish up the braised chicken she'd made to tempt Greta's appetite. There was fresh bread from the *boulangerie*. The kitchen smelled wonderful and felt so cozy with the renewed rain beating on the wide windows in the darkness outside.

Greta's nap and bath had rejuvenated her. She "dressed" for dinner, in that she put on actual clothes and not lounge pajamas. It felt nice to slip a silky sweater over her head and run a comb through her sparse hair. Her slacks were loose on her hips, and she pulled out a pair of ballet flats rather than her slippers.

The chicken was delicious, and she and Beatrice shared the rest of the wine and talked for some time after they had finished eating.

Greta had been thinking a lot about how kind Beatrice was to her. Not just as an employee, but as a kind person and a friend. Never too intrusive, she always respected Greta's privacy. She'd been thinking of putting something in her will to go to Beatrice so that when she died there would be something to help tide her over until she found a new position. But Greta was feeling so optimistic tonight, she'd think more about that another time. There didn't seem to be much hurry, and she'd be seeing her attorney soon anyway about the Sandy thing. Yes, what good was all that money she'd be leaving behind if it didn't help people who had been good to her?

CHAPTER TWELVE

While Greta and Beatrice sipped and chatted away in Presidio Heights, Kestrel huddled miserably in the ancient VW Beetle in the cell phone lot of San Francisco International Airport. She was there to pick up her mother, whom she reflected could easily have hired a car or gotten a shuttle to take her back to her home in Marin. But no, Kestrel thought, it was a matter of loyalty and respect to drag her poor daughter, who had worked two shifts that day, out into the dark and cold to pick her up.

Making it worse was the fact that picking Victoria up had taken on a sliding scale aspect that Kestrel hated. First the flight was due in at 7:00 p.m., then at 7:45, then it had landed but Victoria insisted she needed to "stop by" the duty-free shop on her way to customs. Just getting back into the country was a crapshoot, as well. Depending on how many international flights came in around the same time, the customs lines could be long, and Kestrel had experience getting through customs with her mom before.

"Good morning ma'am, passport, please, and customs declaration." Spoken in a monotone by a uniformed agent.

That is when the fun began. "Is this banana I got on the airplane considered produce? How about this mince pie I got in London from the hotel? What value can I bring into the country without declaring it? How about this shit pile of cash I always travel with and carried all over Europe with me and never spent because I put everything on my credit card for tax purposes?" Okay, the last one was Kestrel's interpretation of her mother's behavior.

She wasn't the only person hanging out in the lot waiting to get the call that their loved one was ready to be picked up, but she was the only one sitting in an ancient VW that leaked and, though the heater worked, you had to keep the car running and stood a chance of running the main gas tank dry and having to switch over to the one-gallon emergency tank since there wasn't a gas gauge. The last time she'd had to do that she'd had to drift into a service station on fumes and almost didn't make it.

Finally, the phone rang. "Where are you? It's cold and raining out here."

"Yes, I know, Mom, I'm in the cell phone lot waiting for your call."

"How far away is that? Why couldn't you just wait at the curb for me?"

"Because they don't let you wait at the curb anymore. It will just take me about ten minutes to get to you."

Victoria sighed. "All right, but I'm not going to wait outside. I'll wait inside where I can sit down. You can park and run in and get me."

Kestrel had started the car and was ready to pull out of the lot. "Mom they won't let me park the car and go in. You'll have to stand inside the door and watch for me. What entrance are you at?"

"The door says Terminal 3, Door 4."

"Okay, I'll be there as soon as I can."

Kestrel hated driving at airports. They were always under construction and nobody knew where they were going. In the dark and rain it was that much worse. When she got to the International Terminal she slowed to watch for the designated entrance. She pulled to a stop and waited, but Victoria didn't come out. One of the heavy-coated and soggy traffic monitors began waving her on and finally came and rapped on her window. She cranked it down, letting the rain pour in.

"Ma'am, you can't park here. You need to move along."

"My mother is right inside, she called me to pick her up. I'm sure she'll be right out."

"You'll have to drive out and come back around. I can't let you sit here."

Just then Victoria came dashing out dragging a rolling suitcase, carrying a purse and three duty-free bags, and balancing a large cup of coffee. "I'm here, I'm here...."

The drenched man looked disgusted and stalked away hunching further down into his coat as Kestrel cranked up the window.

Victoria pulled open the passenger door and tried to release the latch on the seat back. "Aren't you going to help me get my stuff into the backseat?"

"No, Mom. Just stuff it back there and get in."

Kestrel watched for several seconds as Victoria wrangled her bags before putting the car in neutral and setting the emergency brake. It was more painful to watch Victoria than it was to get out and help her, even in the rain.

As soon as Kestrel came around the back of the car Victoria dashed back under the overhang leaving the struggle to Kestrel.

Once Kestrel had safely tucked everything into the backseat, she turned to find her mother chatting amiably with a gentleman standing waiting for his ride and sipping her vente latte delicately, eyelashes batting. "*Okay, Mom*...all set." She spoke loudly and didn't miss the annoyed glance her mother sent her. Did she really have to advertise that Victoria was old enough to have grown children?

The drive in the traffic through San Francisco, up 19th Avenue and across the Golden Gate was congested and fraught with the usual minor accidents and people who'd forgotten how slick the roads could get. Finally they found their way up the dark muddy road to Victoria's home, got her and her luggage into the kitchen, and turned on the heat.

It wasn't really late, but it was dark and cold and Kestrel was tired and beginning to have the nagging back-of-the-eyes headache that long contact with Victoria engendered. "Well, I guess I'll be heading back Mom. Glad you got home safe and sound."

"Don't leave yet. I want to get a pizza and I need you to pick it up."

"Can't you have something delivered? I'm really beat and it will take a while for me to get home."

"You know they never want to deliver out here, and even when they say they will it takes forever and the pizza gets here soggy and cold."

"Okay, okay, just call in the order and I'll go get it now."

While Victoria looked up the number and placed the call Kestrel set the bags up on the kitchen table and wheeled the suitcase into the bedroom. She opened the fridge. Victoria really was going to need to get some food. She'd been gone a couple of weeks and everything looked very sad, except for the open bottle of wine in the door. There was a sour odor emanating from somewhere in the back so Kestrel grabbed the wine bottle and closed the door quickly.

Kestrel could hear her mother's end of the call and did not envy the employee taking her order.

"Yes, I want to order a pizza to be picked up. How small is your small pizza? Really? That doesn't sound large enough. How large is your medium pizza? Hmmm… Okay, a medium, I think. I don't know. How thin is your thin crust? How about the thick crust? How much thicker is the pan pizza than the thick crust? Do you have a gluten-free crust? Oh, only in the small size. Why can't I get gluten free in the medium? Pre-packaged? You don't make it there, it's frozen? Okay, then not the gluten-free. The thick crust, not the pan pizza, a medium. Is there a difference in price between the thin crust and the thicker crust? Okay. I want extra sauce on the pizza, with mushrooms, olives, but not too many, and sausage. Yes, a medium, thick crust pizza with extra sauce, mushrooms, sausage and a few olives. How long will that take? That long? Okay, I will be paying with cash when it is picked up. Why do you need my phone number? I don't really like to give it out. I will be sending someone to pick it up. Her name is Kestrel Jonas." Finally, she hung up the phone and Kestrel felt she was almost as relieved as the pizza person surely was.

"Oh no, I forgot to tell them I wanted cheese on the pizza."

"Mom, everyone always puts cheese on the pizza unless you specifically tell them not to."

"No, I don't want it without cheese. I'm going to have to call them back."

Kestrel picked up her refilled wineglass and wandered into the living room to avoid hearing the second call.

Several minutes later her mother joined her. "They say it will take half an hour before you can pick it up. Help me put some of this stuff away."

By the time they had stashed away the various expensive skin creams bought duty-free and pulled the undeclared items from the hidden pockets in the suitcase, it was time to go get the pizza. At least the place wasn't far away. When Kestrel gave her name the person at the counter gave her a look. "I know, that was my mother. Take this for your trouble." She added a $20 bill to the payment and scurried out the door.

CHAPTER THIRTEEN

Beatrice carefully folded the unicorn hood scarves she'd knitted for her girls into layers of tissue paper and placed them in the gift bags. The twins did not like to dress alike and had been known to switch their clothes and try to pass for one another around people who didn't know them as well as Beatrice did. Lucy had a darling dimple in the lower part of her left cheek, and Lisbeth's lashes were much longer. Beatrice thought she was better at telling them apart than their own mother was. She had carefully knitted the hoods exactly the same except for being in different colors so that they would have nothing to fight about. She knew that none of their friends would have anything like them.

She had been hired by the Spencers with glowing references from former employers in New York City when she first moved to San Francisco and the girls were only babies. Oh, they had been a handful. They were such little monkeys that, at one point, the only furnishings in their nursery had been two mattresses placed on the floor. Anything that could be climbed on, turned over, emptied, or taken apart had to be removed for their safety and everyone else's sanity.

Now they were in school and didn't need a full-time nanny, and when the Spencers divorced Beatrice had been let go. Now they spent Wednesday through Saturday with their mother and Sunday through Tuesday with their father and new mommy.

At first Sharon Spencer had not wanted to let Beatrice see them, but when she realized that Beatrice was willing to take responsibility for them for entire Saturdays she'd warmed up to the idea.

When Sharon Spencer found something that benefited her she was unlikely to ask many questions. For example, the fact that Beatrice's passport and driver's license claimed that she was forty-five years old, but she could pass for thirty-ish, which she actually was, didn't bother Mrs. Spencer a bit, although she had hinted a few times that she was curious about Beatrice's skin care routine.

Greta allowed Beatrice to take her car on Saturdays so she didn't have to take the bus and could take the girls on little trips without having to worry about the weather. The rain had stopped but the clouds still hung low over the city. Today she was going to take them to a tea shop in Ghirardelli Square for a lovely afternoon tea served with tiny sandwiches and cakes, and they would end the trip at the chocolate shop. Beatrice wondered if she would ever have little girls of her own to have lovely adventures with. But, for now, she would hug them and spoil them, and make sure they understood what was important in life beyond privilege and money. For now, they would start their outing with her saying, "So, what kind of mischief should we get into today?"

That was what her Aunt Beatrice used to say to her when they would set out on their adventures in New York City. Auntie Bea was only fifteen years older than Beatrice, the younger sister of her mother, and Beatrice, then known as Betty, had gone to live with her aunt when she was twenty years old. They had looked much alike, as did all the women of her family, and would sometimes dress alike and tell people that they were sisters. Auntie Bea was a naturalized citizen who had lived in the States since she was a young woman. She had no children and enjoyed having her niece with her. They had moved to San Francisco when Auntie Bea got sick. Before she passed, they'd made a plan that had changed Beatrice's life.

Today, though, would not be life changing. It would be fun, and frivolous, and end with all of them running on a sugar high. If their mother had plans that evening, then Beatrice would spend the night with them and return to Walnut Street on Sunday morning.

Greta had risen early and spent an unusual amount of time dressing and putting on makeup. Thankfully, the treatment given her on the clinical trial had not caused her to lose all her hair but she still owned several expensive wigs that she wore when she went out, and she spent some time deciding which to wear today. She wandered through the house straightening items that were a bit out of place, but happy that Beatrice kept things neat and dusted. She'd made a pot of coffee and set out a simple plate of cheeses and fruit with a bottle of sparkling wine in the chiller, in case she wanted it later. It surprised her how excited she was to be welcoming a visitor on her own; in fact it was energizing and felt oddly normal that she was on her own. It had been a while since she felt independent and truly interested in the day. To tamp down her nerves she'd even turned on the news and listened for a bit. It was amazing how you could not listen to the news or read a paper for an extended period of time and still feel like the same old crap was going on the same old way when you went back to it. She remembered when she was first married she'd been a fan of a couple of soap operas, and then got busy with life and stopped watching them. When she'd been in bed after her last miscarriage she turned them back on after years away, and there were the same actors doing the same crap to each other. One of them had moved from one show to another and even changed networks, but she was still lying and cheating the same way. Same shit, different day, town, and network.

Watching the news also kept her from standing next to the window peering out onto the street anxiously awaiting her guest. She knew from experience that the interminable gazing into the street only made the tension worse.

She'd just focused on a mayoral news conference when the doorbell finally chimed, startling her and bringing a flush to her cheeks.

She rushed to the door but then stopped to peer into the mirror in the entry. She wondered briefly if she'd overdone the makeup. Blusher always made her feel clownish, but it was too late now. She did pull a tissue from her pocket and scrub some of the rosy hue from her cheeks.

In a way that made it worse because it reddened her own complexion, as well.

Opening the door, she noted that the rain clouds had cleared away and wan winter sunshine spilled through onto the tiled floor. "Sandeep, welcome."

"Ms. Gardner, so good to see you." Sandy hesitated on the step as Greta stood back so he could enter. Taking this step was unprecedented for him and taking it would change things.

"Welcome to my home. Please come in."

He had thought to bring a hostess gift of some kind. Flowers, or wine, or maybe candy, but reminded himself that he was here in an official, if unsanctioned, capacity. "Thank you. This is a lovely neighborhood. I don't get to Presidio Heights often." Only when he walked through the elite neighborhoods of the city thinking what it would be like if he were able to live here instead of in his shared apartment near Dolores Park.

"I've almost always lived in this house. It belonged to my parents and after they passed away my first husband and I moved into it. I felt I was so lucky to be the only heir so that it didn't have to be sold and divided up among the relatives." Greta had continued on into the living room.

Following her, Sandy noted the large window looking out on a view of the San Francisco Bay. This is the way that he should be living.

Greta gestured toward the best seat in the room, the wing backed chair facing the view. "Please, sit down. I've made some coffee and I'm quite excited to hear how my tests turned out."

Sandy sat in the proffered chair and set the briefcase he carried down next to it. He had test results and papers he could show her, but he'd pored over the documents and didn't need them to convey the news.

"Yes, I'm really happy to tell you that your treatment seems to be giving some exciting results. In fact, the doctors are rather amazed at the progress they show."

Greta's heart leapt, much as Sandy's had sunk, at the news. "That's wonderful. But I don't really know what that means. Please explain in layman's terms."

"Well, basically, it means that they've seen substantial shrinkage of the primary and metastatic tumors and your CTCs are almost non-detectable."

"CTCs?"

"Those are Circulating Tumor Cells. Kind of free-floating cells that have been cast off from the cancer and are floating around in your bloodstream. Your initial numbers were high, but now they can barely be detected. It's one of the endpoints for the study."

"That's wonderful, I guess. But what does it mean for me?"

"Yes, yes, it is wonderful. It is still early, but it looks like that continued treatment could greatly extend your life-expectancy."

Greta, who'd been sitting on the edge of the love seat, sat back. She'd rather expected good news from the way Sandy had spoken on the phone but wasn't quite sure how to process what he had told her. She'd spent the past few months trying to come to grips with the idea that she was going to die, sooner or later, as we all did, but that sooner seemed like the greater probability. After a few moments she spoke. "I don't know what to say."

"I understand, Ms. Gardner."

"Please call me Greta. Anyone who comes with such a lovely gift should definitely use my first name. In fact, I have some champagne chilling and I feel like celebrating."

CHAPTER FOURTEEN

Greta went to the kitchen to get the wine and glasses, and Sandeep took the opportunity to look around the room a bit. The house was old but had been updated a bit with good heating and air conditioning, though you seldom needed the latter in San Francisco. The furniture was good quality but not new. His mother had told him once that you should never buy really expensive household items as they lasted long past your wanting to keep them. "Buy mid-range," she'd said. "Then, when you get tired of them and they are starting to look shabby, you don't feel guilty replacing them." He could see that Greta was a victim of furniture that would probably outlast her. He heard Greta coming back from the kitchen and returned to the wingback chair.

They toasted to her good news, chatted for a while, and finished the bottle of champagne. Greta was surprised how charming Sandeep could be. Laughing at her little jokes and flattering her in a way that she knew was gratuitous, but was welcome, nonetheless.

Greta looked at the empty bottle. She would like a bit more but thought better of opening a new bottle. "Would you like to see the rest of the house?"

Sandy had been trying to think of a good way to broach the subject of a tour and jumped at the chance. "I would love to. It is such a lovely, classic San Francisco residence."

They toured the downstairs and Greta navigated the stairs to the second floor with a bit of a wobble. Maybe she'd had more of the wine than she thought. Had Sandeep even taken a second glass?

"This is the primary bedroom, my room."

Sandeep started suddenly. "Did you hear someone downstairs?"

Then a voice called out. "Hello, Greta. Don't be startled, I am just here to pick up some items so I can spend the night with the girls." It was Beatrice and her charges. The chattering voices of Lisbeth and Lucy rose up the stairs.

"Don't worry, it is only Beatrice, my companion."

"I know, but it really isn't seemly for me to be here alone with you."

Greta laughed lightly at the old-fashioned notion. "Don't be silly, Sandy, there's nothing going on."

"Yes, of course. But it is professionally not appropriate. Can you see that she doesn't know that I am here?"

"Of course." Greta glanced around the room as she heard Beatrice start up the stairs. "I'm up here, Beatrice. I'll be down in a moment." To Sandeep, "Just duck into the bathroom there and close the door."

The bathroom door closed just before Beatrice entered the bedroom. "There you are. Mrs. Spencer asked if I could stay the night with the girls. I hope you don't mind. We're going to have a little slumber party."

"No, of course not. I just wasn't expecting you until later." Greta's face looked a little flushed and Beatrice glanced around the room.

"I saw that there was a wine bottle and glasses in the dining room. Did Mr. Frankel come by for a visit?"

"What? Oh yes, Bertie was here for a bit. I probably shouldn't have been drinking in the middle of the day, but I have been feeling so well... I was just thinking I would take a little nap."

Beatrice paused for a moment, but the chatter and giggling of the girls on the stairs distracted her from whatever she was about to ask.

"There are leftovers from last night. I will just make you up a plate that you can pop into the microwave. Are you sure you will be okay overnight?"

"Of course, Bea. I told you I am feeling much better this week."

A loud shriek and giggles from the stairway drew Beatrice out the door. "You girls behave yourselves. Ms. Gardner is going to think you are little terrors." She turned back to Greta. "I'll will just get my things and make up a dinner plate, then we'll be off. You have my cell phone number if you need me. I can be back in in fifteen minutes if you call."

"Beatrice, I shall be fine. Now go along and shut the door behind you. I'm going to lie down for a bit."

Beatrice closed the bedroom door and followed the sound of giggling down the stairs.

It took just a few minutes for Beatrice to gather up her things and fix a plate. She picked up the empty wine bottle and glasses on her way through the living room and noted the unfamiliar briefcase still sitting next to the wingbacked chair. She thought Bertie must have left it behind so she left it where it was so he could find it when he returned. Odd, though. She'd never seen him carry a briefcase before. He'd left umbrellas, gloves, and once his hat, behind. But never a briefcase.

Greta stood at the bedroom window and watched Beatrice pull the car out of the driveway and head down Walnut Street before she moved to the bathroom door and tapped gently. "Sandy, she's gone. You can come out."

Sandy had not wasted his hiding time. American homes were a matter of great interest to him under normal circumstances, but the rich in general and Greta in particular were fascinating. Her bath for example. She had both a roomy shower and a gigantic, jetted tub. The shelf in the shower and the ledge around the tub were full of products, each of which he examined without touching them. Sugar scrub, shampoo, conditioner, body wash, loofahs, razors, and fluffy shower puffs made of mesh in the shower. Around the tub: scented oils and candles, bubble bath, long-handled brushes, lotions, and the one jarring item, a brass Aladdin's lamp. He lifted the lid of the lamp and the strong odor of burnt incense rose up to meet him. He could see the residue of a previously burnt cone and, looking around, saw that the edge of the tub also held a glass jar full of incense. He shook his head. For him, bathing was a necessity, a task that was best done with thoroughness and dispatch. He didn't know if it was a female thing to make such a fuss of it, or if Greta did this because she could afford to.

He'd glanced through the medicine cabinet, opened the vanity drawers, looked into the cabinets under the sink. There was not much of interest there. He had seen that some of Greta's medications were on the nightstand next to her bed and assumed that others were in the tiny drawer in the stand. The bathroom was well stocked with fresh towels, toilet paper, air freshener spray, and wet wipes. He picked up a small spray bottle from the back of the toilet. It instructed the user to spray the contents onto the top of the water in the toilet before use, presumably to keep down odors. Going to the toilet was apparently a bigger occasion for her than it was for him.

When Greta tapped on the door he slid closed the drawer he'd been looking through and opened the door. "Thanks for covering for me. It probably is not totally professional for me to be here drinking champagne with one of my study subjects."

"It was no problem. Beatrice just wanted to let me know that she'd be gone until tomorrow morning. She needed to pick up a couple of things." Greta didn't really know what to say after that.

Sandy looked uncomfortable, as well. "I guess I should probably get going. I've taken up your whole day."

"There's no rush. We could order in some dinner if you like."

"Actually, I really should go. Things I need to do at home."

"Of course. Silly me, you probably have a date on Saturday night."

"No, no date. Just some work I need to catch up on before that study monitor comes back on Monday."

"Ah, always working. You work too much, already."

Greta led him back downstairs and he gathered up his briefcase. She noted that the champagne bottle and glasses had been removed. "Beatrice probably thought it was strange that I'd been down here drinking champagne on a Saturday afternoon. Oh well, when the cat's away, the mice will play."

"I'm sorry…the cat?"

"Oh, it's just a silly American saying. Nothing really."

When Sandy had left Greta felt strangely lonely and thought about who she might call to have a bit of gossip with, but she couldn't think of a single soul. Company in the afternoon had been lovely but now the house seemed terribly empty and cold. After a bit she went into the kitchen and made a pot of tea. She took it upstairs and set it next to her bed, then put on her coziest jammies, and opening the safe, removed a folder of papers from it. She spent the rest of the evening in one of her favorite pastimes, spending her money. She'd been rethinking her will and estate lately. She hadn't wanted to dwell on her death, but now that the news was so good, she felt a thrill of enthusiasm at the idea of redistributing her money. It was like taking a big shopping trip. Figuring out the value of your estate and how it could be distributed after you were gone. She'd never had any children and really had no family, but there were lots of people that she would love to surprise with a bequest. Of course, there were people she would surprise by the lack of a bequest, as well. She'd already talked to Sandy about his foundation and what she could do to help him establish his medical practice in the United States. Bertie had been a stalwart friend forever, and, though she was sure he wasn't expecting it, she wanted to leave him some money to make his life as easy as possible. Of course, he was not that young and had no family either, so it was interesting to ponder where the money would go from him. It was like ripples on a pond, spreading ever outward.

She'd also been giving some thought to Beatrice. Of course, she really was paid help, but she was a sweet and loving person and Greta could certainly afford to be generous. She wondered what Beatrice would do with money if she had a substantial chunk. Maybe she would go back to Jamaica, although she seemed perfectly happy here, and her darling girls were in San Francisco.

She opened her laptop and checked on her various investments and holdings. She wasn't nearly the ninny some people thought she was when it came to money. Money just didn't take a lot of her time. What was there to think about when there'd always been plenty for anything you wanted or needed?

At the Spencer home Beatrice and the girls had made grilled cheese and tomato soup for dinner, dunking the triangles of sandwich into the soup, and made a big bowl of popcorn to eat while they watched Disney movies. At bedtime they'd played the girls' favorite game, "Tell me about when I was a baby."

Beatrice had so many funny and cute stories about the girls and she remembered them all. Quite honestly, the girls remembered them, as well, since Beatrice had told them again and again. But they never tired of hearing about the cute, silly, or downright mischievous things they had done when they were younger.

CHAPTER FIFTEEN

Kestrel Jonas clocked out at the Pacific Union Club where she'd worked the dinner shift and caught the bus for home. It wasn't late but the rain had continued to pour. She must have ten umbrellas at home but never one with her when she needed it. Her gym bag contained makeup, changes of clothes including stiletto heels and Gucci sunglasses, personal notes that amounted to a Who's Who of the whole city, brochures for a planned vacation in Hawaii, snack bars, bags of nuts, two overdue library books, cannabis gummies, chocolate, and a notebook and pen that allowed her to take notes and record the conversations connected to them. But, no umbrella, poncho, plastic bag, or anything else that could have kept her from getting completely soaked on her way up the hill from the bus stop to her duplex on Bay Street. At least the bag itself was waterproof, although it was too hefty to carry above her head for protection. She vowed to herself that as soon as she got home she would immediately put one of the collapsible umbrellas in the bag.

By the time she had checked her mail, opened a bottle of wine, wiped up the puddle of water from the floor, and wrapped a towel around her head she had forgotten all about her vow.

She considered opening a bag of chips since the staff meal before dinner service had been several hours ago but decided she'd rather use her calories for an extra glass of wine.

She was grateful that she had forgotten to turn off the heat when she left early that morning, although her mother, her landlady, kept close track of the utility use and was sure to mention the bill this month. This was one of the days when she'd worked two shifts at two different private dining rooms and she was chilled and tired.

In the past she'd worked the breakfast and lunch shift at the elite, private Pacific Union Club on Nob Hill and dinners at The Towers, an exclusive and expensive retirement community. But she'd recently determined that the juiciest gossip at the PU Club happened in the evening and the elderly residents of The Towers were more alert and chattier earlier in the day. So, she'd arranged to switch her shifts. Nobody there really cared and she needed a constant stream of interesting tidbits to keep her blog, *SFUndertheRug.com*, intriguing and viable.

She'd used the time on the bus to check messages on her two cell phones: the burner phone that held mostly cat videos and messages from her mother, Victoria, and the one that usually stayed tucked in her tummy-control panties except when she was snapping pictures and recording quiet conversations for later review and use on social media.

Initially, picking up bits of gossip and scandal on the privileged people she waited on had been a kind of fun and interesting way to spice up her own dull life. After college she'd taken some low-paying jobs at various venues in San Francisco just to keep the wolf away from the door. Thankfully, her mother let her rent one side of a duplex she owned in Noe Valley at a reduced rate, although it rankled her terribly that Kestrel wasn't using that expensive—all right, mid-range—college degree Victoria had paid for. (Technically, Victoria's mother had left the money for it, but there was no need to tell Kestrel that.)

When Kestrel's nose for news landed her in a vat of hot water her friend, Inspector Bobby Burns, had asked her why she had it in for rich folks. She really couldn't say, except that their attitude of entitlement rankled her and she loved to deflate them, just a little bit, if she got the chance. The police commissioner had not seen the quirky side of the blog when his elaborate Tinkertoy system of personal checks and balances, usually bank balances, came under scrutiny because of her posts.

There was not much of interest in the messages she had now. Mostly they were hang-ups, but one call from her friend Beatrice had piqued her interest. This particular friend was a font of inside information on the wealthy. Bea would probably just be getting Greta into bed and settled for the evening now. Kestrel would call her tomorrow.

Kestrel couldn't hear the music from the other side of the duplex but the steady thump of the bass told her that her neighbor, Sam, was working. He listened to heavy rock and roll when he worked and smooth jazz when he was relaxing.

An email pinged in with an update on her portfolio, which she never looked at except for the bottom line, that just seemed to be going up and up. The seven-figure totals didn't hold much reality for her. Historically her bank balance hovered much lower, but she'd come into a little money she wasn't quite sure what to do with, so she just let it do its own thing, except for that trip to Hawaii that she was going to take as soon as she got the chance. The frigid rain outside and meager heat coming from the floor register in the kitchen made a warm climate sound better and better.

One of the cell phones rang and a picture of Bobby Burns popped up on the screen.

"Hey, Bobby. What's up?"

"Not much. How about you?"

"Same." She waited, Bobby didn't just call for no reason even when they'd been dating, so she was sure he had something on his mind now.

"Say, I just had a question for you…because you're a girl and all."

"Really, I thought you'd forgotten I was a girl." This was getting interesting.

"Very funny. I just don't know what to think about Rocky."

"Ah, Rocky. Well, she's a tough one, I will admit that."

"You're telling me." He paused for a beat or two. "You know we've been kind of going out since her transfer to Fraud came through."

"Yeah, I heard that."

"You did? From who?"

"It's just a saying, Bobby. I know you are dating. So what?"

"Well, it's just, like tonight. She's having dinner in Oakland with her family and she made it pretty clear she didn't want me to come."

"How did she make it clear?"

"For one thing she didn't invite me."

"Ah..." The word hung on the line between them.

"I mean, it's been a few months and I've never met them. I don't even know if they know about me. She never talks about them; I hardly know their names."

"What's your question, Bobby?"

"That's it, why doesn't she want me to meet her family?"

Kestrel grinned; she loved yanking his chain. "Could it be because you are a homicide cop, or maybe because you're a white boy?"

"She was in homicide before she was in Fraud." His voice was indignant. "...And why would they care if I'm white? I don't care that they're Black."

Kestrel sighed. "Maybe she just worries that you or they will be uncomfortable. Give it time, Bobby. She could dump you any day and you'll have wasted all this time worrying about it."

There was silence on the other end of the phone.

"I'll tell you what, why don't you come over here and have a glass of wine, or three. I'm just having some and I don't have to work in the morning. I'll even throw in a frozen dinner for you."

"Yeah, well, maybe. I'll text you if I decide to come over."

"Whatever." And Kestrel hung up the phone.

Bobby sounded like he thought she was luring him into her den of iniquity to jump his bones. Been there, done that, don't need to go there again, she thought.

CHAPTER SIXTEEN

Of course, each of the girls had her own bedroom, but when Beatrice stayed with them they both slept in one of the rooms, often with Beatrice sitting and rocking in a chair next to them. Their regular bedtimes were not important on those special days, but they usually were tired and before too long the giggling and whispering would stop and they would drift off to sleep. Beatrice would often wake late in the night still sitting in the chair and make her way to the other girl's empty bedroom.

In the morning she would wash and dry the sheets from the bed she'd used, make sure everything had been picked up from the night before and, after assuring that Mrs. Spencer was in the house, she'd slip away before the girls woke up.

On Sunday morning she returned to the Gardner home, put the car in the garage, and let herself in through the kitchen. It didn't look like Greta had made or ordered dinner, and the glasses, wine bottle, and plate with remnants of cheese, fruit and crackers still sat on the counter.

She returned her overnight bag to her downstairs bedroom and straightened the kitchen, then she quietly went up the stairs and peeked in on Greta. She had fallen asleep with the laptop and some papers scattered across the duvet. A pot of cold tea and a small plate with a few telltale cookie crumbs sat on the nightstand. Beatrice slipped into the room and picked up the pot and plate, leaving the papers where they were. She'd noticed that the wall safe was open and assumed the papers were personal. Greta would put them away when she woke up.

Going down the stairs, she was happy to think of Greta having the energy and interest to take care of business. For a while she'd been failing but seemed to feel better and more optimistic now.

As Beatrice puttered around the house, putting things in order and jotting down notes on what needed buying, fixing, or cleaning, her mind wandered to what she would do when Greta didn't need her anymore. She focused on when Greta got well rather than when she might die. It felt very wrong to be bringing negative energy into the space. After all, things seemed to be going so much better now. Still, if Greta got well she wouldn't need a companion and Beatrice would be looking for a job, again.

Would she stay in San Francisco or should she go someplace else? She purposely had not made a lot of close friends here. Her past and the jeopardy she would be in if anyone found out made it dangerous to let people get too close. Sometimes it was lonely, though.

She wasn't sure what would happen if people knew the truth, but she knew she couldn't go back to Jamaica. There was nothing and no one there for her now.

She was startled when her phone rang and she saw that Kestrel was calling. "Hello, how are you, Kestrel?"

"Good, I'm really good. How about you?"

"Very good, as well."

"So did you get any information on what Annabelle Leigh was doing visiting Greta?"

"Not really. I think the two of them had been thick as thieves growing up and then had a falling out over Bertie Frankel, who just happened to be married to Annabelle."

"Really, fighting over Bertie Frankel? I can't quite picture it myself."

Beatrice laughed, "Me, either."

"I did some checking around and there was quite a hubbub over it all back in the day."

"Everything seems to have settled down now. There is something interesting, though. Maybe you could put something in the blog about how wonderfully Ms. Gardner is doing. She always reads your blog and would be tickled pink to have her name show up in it."

"I will. I'm glad she's doing better."

"Maybe having her name out there will remind some of her friends to come visit."

"It can't hurt anything. I'll let you go but give me a call if anything interesting turns up. The rich and famous of San Francisco have been behaving themselves lately and it is making it very hard on me."

"I'm sure it won't last long."

When they'd finished their call Beatrice made her way up the stairs to Greta's room. The older woman had tucked everything back in the safe and closed her laptop. She could hear the quiet snuffle and buzz of the robot vacuum cleaner in the hallway. Beatrice thought the little device was a wonder. Periodically, it slid out of its little house under the wardrobe and methodically made its way around the open rooms picking up all the mess, then slipped back into its hidey-hole to recharge.

"Beatrice, I was just about to ring you for some breakfast. Do we have any of those lovely scones you baked the other morning?"

"Of course, and I have some clotted cream and jam I think you'll like. I can bring some up right away."

"Lovely. You know, maybe we could get out of the house later today. I haven't been anywhere but the clinic in months and I see that San Francisco is glistening in the sunshine today."

"Sure, we could go for a Sunday drive. Maybe take a picnic."

"A picnic… I thought I'd never go on another one in my life, but you never know what the future will bring. We could go to Golden Gate Park. Don't forget I have a handicapped pass for parking."

They both laughed at that and Beatrice found herself humming as she went down the stairs.

CHAPTER SEVENTEEN

Sunita scowled at the butter chicken recipe on her tablet, not sure what a "pinch" of turmeric meant. Why couldn't Sandeep's mother just say how much of a spice to use rather than torment her with a dash, a pinch, and a smidgeon here and there. She suspected the recipe wasn't even the one that Sandeep had such fond memories of. This wouldn't be the first time that she had labored over an elaborate meal that didn't meet his high expectations.

The drone from the living room reminded her that one of her better ideas had been to subscribe to ESPN+ so that Sandeep could lounge on her sofa and listen to endless cricket matches. His roommates watched American football, basketball, hockey, and baseball, but had never learned to love cricket the way he did. Her brothers had played when she was a child, but she had never cared for sports. Still, it lured him to her apartment on a regular basis, so it was worth it.

She allowed herself a moment of annoyance that it never occurred to him to take her out for a meal. She made more money than he and would have been delighted to pay for the meal, but it would take some thought on his part and she suspected his favorite part of their relationship was that he had to make absolutely no effort.

As the spicy sauce simmered on the cooktop she stepped to the doorway to the living room. "Do you need another beer, or some tea?"

He picked up the empty beer bottle and waggled it in her direction as his response, his eyes still fixed on the television screen.

Sunita opened the refrigerator and pulled a bottle of Kingfisher beer from its depths. Another special purchase that went unappreciated.

"How is the match going?"

Sandeep's only response was an irritated shrug. He never liked to talk during the match.

She sat down next to him and he dropped his arm across her shoulders as she feigned interest in the game playing out on the huge TV that she almost never watched. Another purchase she'd made to please him.

The sun shone outside and there was a new exhibit at the de Young Museum, but she would take walks and go to museums once she and Sandeep were married. If his team won the match today she might broach the subject over dinner. Her parents had broadly hinted that she was not getting any younger and had threatened to approach Wedding Alliances, an Indian marriage bureau.

They were proud of her career. Trained as a chemist, she had moved on to get an MBA in finance and landed a prestigious job at UCSF Medical Center, where she'd met Sandeep when he began working there. But, her brothers and sister were now all married and she was on the shady side of thirty years of age. The time was ripe to marry. Sandeep was good-looking and could be very charming, not that he wasted his efforts on her. She wondered idly if she should mention the marriage bureau to him. How would he respond? Would it worry him at all?

The conversation over dinner was encouraging.

"I went to see Ms. Gardner today to tell her about her test results."

"Ms. Gardner, she is the one who lives in Presidio Heights. How is she?" Sunita tried to sound caring.

"She is doing well. Much too well, in fact. Her house is old-fashioned but it is a huge place for just one sick woman and her servant. It is the kind of place I should live in."

Sunita ignored the reference to only himself. She'd pretend he meant it was the sort of place "we" should live in.

"Of course, her private bathroom is ridiculous. A bathtub big enough for several people and all kinds of candles, incense, bubbles…she must spend half her life in there."

"Why would you have been in her private bathroom?" She tried to sound mildly curious rather than suspicious.

"I had to duck in there when her woman came home unexpectedly. I didn't want anyone to know I was there." Sandeep shrugged off any further questions and concentrated on his meal.

Dinner had been more successful than she'd feared and the cricket match had ended well. She was clearing the table as he leaned back in his chair.

"Mummy and Papa called last night. They were asking me about a marriage bureau. Mummy said that there are many here in the United States."

"Why are they asking about a marriage bureau? What is the hurry to marry, you are doing well in your career. Can't that be enough for now?" He sounded irritated, but she couldn't decide if it was because he thought he might have competition or because he thought she was pushing him.

"They just want me to be settled, to have my own family, like my brothers and my sister."

"Have you told them that we have discussed marriage?"

"Certainly not. If I even mentioned you to them they would begin making plans. They would be flying here to meet you and contacting your parents."

Sandeep paled at the thought. "That is good. We will talk to them when the time is right."

"When will the time be right, Sandeep?"

"When the money is good. They won't want you to marry a broke maybe-doctor. I would be ashamed to have them see my apartment and know how little money I make."

"But, I don't care about that, I make money and my family has money."

"I do care about it. I would be shamed in front of your brothers."

Sunita hesitated, but then blurted, "But you always say that things must change, but they never do change. When will they change?"

She could tell she had pushed too hard as he stood abruptly and looked at his watch.

"I must be going. This conversation will have to wait for another day."

She could tell that he was angry, but she was also becoming angry. She knew he wasn't seeing anyone else, except for his "aunties" at the cancer center. The ones that fawned over him and left him money when they died their miserable deaths.

The tears of frustration did not come until he had gone home, but they did come. They came so often after he left. He did not want to marry, or did not want to marry her, but she still hoped to find a way to make it happen. There must be a way. She'd jeopardized her job and her reputation by feeding him financial information on the aunties so that he didn't waste his charm on someone who could not benefit him. She had helped him set up his foundation so that money could be funneled to him when they died, she dressed well, she was doting, she was patient, but she couldn't make her skin fairer, her hair more lustrous, herself younger. Working out, spending money, cooking, waiting on his desires, none of it was working. Of course, she wanted him to love her, but she would settle for him marrying her.

Sunita looked into the mirror and squinted her eyes to remove some years from the image. She knew she wasn't glamorous, or sexy. She was okay to look at but she was meticulous with her wardrobe and makeup. Still, a number of years had crept by since she'd finished college and gone to work at the university.

Sunita didn't drink but she considered opening some of the wine she kept on hand in case Sandeep wanted it. She opened a bottle and poured a glass but didn't really like the taste. The glass sat next to her on the table as the apartment grew dark and she pondered how to make Sandeep agree to marry. When the apartment had grown completely dark she poured out the wine and went to bed. Maybe an idea would come to her in her sleep.

CHAPTER EIGHTEEN

Bertie settled himself into the comfy booth in the dark restaurant. The damask-covered cushion groaned slightly beneath his bulk. Thinking back, he could recall that he and Annabelle had dined here a number of times when they were courting, or dating, or hooking up, back in the day. Was courting even a word anymore? Was it even still in use then? Never mind. The nostalgia of the place was one of the reasons that he'd picked this particular restaurant.

The original owners had given way to their children long ago and now it was probably run by grandchildren, or a corporation. It had the cachet of the old seafood places at Fisherman's Wharf. Those famous landmarks had been serving San Francisco for decades, and gradually the food had gotten more expensive and less tasty. The last time he'd gone to the Wharf it was crowded, loud, and the food was ghastly.

He at least hoped that this old place could still turn out a decent prime rib and baked potato with a nice wedge salad. He hoped that

Annabelle had not given over her lifestyle to the popular disdain of red meat.

He picked up the wine list and his spirits also picked up. At least their wine buyers had some taste.

He'd come a bit early hoping to impress the sommelier with his knowledge of fine wines. He wasn't as concerned with ordering the best, as he was with demonstrating that he knew what the best was, even if he couldn't afford it.

He ordered cocktails to be brought as soon as his guest arrived, a Bombay Sapphire martini for him, and a Maker's Mark 46 Manhattan with extra cherries for her. He remembered that Annabelle only drank white wines, even with prime rib, so compromised with a bottle of mid-range Sauvignon Blanc to be served with their meal.

The restaurant was quiet, so each opening of the heavy door ushered in a swoosh of street noise, and it was with one of these swooshes that Annabelle entered the dining room.

She was backlit by the window and for a moment she looked almost as she had so many years ago. Truth be told, she looked better, more sophisticated and polished. The lighting was dim and forgiving and he hoped that he was served as well by it as she was.

"Bertie, you are looking as debonair as ever." She stepped to the table and dropped a light kiss on his cheek before sliding into the booth across from him. He wondered for a moment if "debonair" was the compliment it once was.

"And you, my dear, are breathtaking. Just looking at you makes me feel decades younger."

"It is all due to money and pampering, I assure you." She laughed lightly as she settled into the soft upholstery.

Her shapewear-snugged bottom had barely settled in the seat before the waiter appeared with the cocktails. At least the service had stayed the same over the years.

"I am surprised you remembered that this is where we had our last lovely dinner together." She said, looking down to smooth the napkin in her lap before picking up the potent drink and taking her first sip, eyeing him over the rim of the glass.

Damn, he'd forgotten that this is where she had told him she was divorcing him. It might have been in this very booth.

"Don't look so sheepish, my dear. That was long ago and, if I recall, we had both had a lot of alcohol." Her smile was reassuring.

"I have to admit, I only have hazy memories of that night…and deep regrets."

"I always think that the best way to expunge a bad memory is to replace it with a good one, and that is what I am bent on doing tonight."

They both settled on their usual order here: the light prime rib meal, with baked potato, and starting with a wedge salad for her; a heftier portion of the perfectly cooked beef for him, with mashed potatoes, creamed spinach, and a dozen briny fresh oysters to start.

It was surprising how comfortable you could be with a long-ago friend even after so many years, as long as you danced delicately around the most obvious reasons that it had been so many years.

They were finishing off the wine when the discussion turned more serious.

"I've been to visit Greta, you know."

"Yes, she did tell me she'd seen you."

"So, you are still in close touch with her?"

"I've tried to be there for her as a friend since she has been ill."

"Of course…" The words hung in the air for several seconds.

Bertie looked around for the waiter. "Maybe we should have another bottle of wine."

"No, I think we should get out of here. Your place or mine, as they used to say."

When Bertie didn't respond she reached over and patted the back of his hand. "You settle the bill and I will phone for an Uber and run to the ladies' room." With that she stood up and walked away, leaving him as his old mother would have said, gobsmacked.

CHAPTER NINETEEN

Bertie was surprised to find that Annabelle had given the driver his address. If he'd expected to have company he'd have been a little tidier in his preparations for going out. Actually, he would not have been tidier, but he would have asked his cleaner to stop by and do a quick dust-up while he was out.

Without a prior heads-up, his bachelor pad looked a bit littered, but Annabelle didn't appear put out. After all, she'd lived with the man for years and the litter of take-out containers, empty glasses, newspapers, and stray socks was not that much of a shock. She might have been more surprised if he had gotten tidier over the years.

Bertie was oblivious to how comfortable he was with a woman being in control of his activities. On his own he sort of just "bobbed along," as his mother used to say.

He left Annabelle to sort herself out in the living room and wandered off to the wine cellar on a quest for something suitable for whatever it was they were doing. He wasn't quite sure what that might be but trusted that he had a bottle of something that might suffice.

It was strange how having someone new in the house made him more aware of how shoddy it had become since he'd inherited it. Someone came regularly to clean the surfaces, of course; counters, tabletops, carpets, and floors were well maintained, but nothing had really been upgraded in years.

It was a pretty common phenomenon in a city where the long-entrenched residents were protected by laws that made it cheaper to stay in their paid-off, oversized properties, without making the improvements they needed.

There was no mortgage to pay and the taxes stayed low, so it made sense, but meant that there were a lot of older people doddering around big family homes as the walls crumbled around them.

Annabelle glanced around the living room and decided the best spot for the discussion she'd planned would be the slightly tattered love seat in front of the picture window. She didn't snoop around the way she had at Greta's because Bertie's house was just a means to an end, the end being taking over Greta's life.

She'd given a lot of thought to how best to enlist Bertie's acquiescence, if not his enthusiasm, in her plan.

Bertie came back into the room with an ice bucket, a bottle of champagne, and two flutes, the crystal ones that his mother had always used. "Look what I found! A long-forgotten bottle of champers from the old days. How better to celebrate our reconnection."

The champagne was more appropriate than Annabelle could have asked, although Bertie didn't know it yet. "Perfect, Bertie. Perfect."

"I'll just leave it here to chill for a few minutes. It's cool in the cellar, but we want it at the perfect forty-eight degrees. Should take about twenty minutes." He set the chilling bucket on the end table and took his seat next to Annabelle.

Annabelle had loosened her scarf a bit and was gratified to note the appreciative glance her cleavage received from her ex-husband. She stretched her arms above her head and leaned forward a bit, to enhance the view. "Being here reminds me of so many good times we had. Sometimes I forget what a nice life we had together. It is good to be here, again."

Bertie glanced around him. He, too, had forgotten how pleasant much of their marriage had been. He frowned for a moment, trying to recall why they had broken up.

Annabelle glimpsed the look of consternation on his face and switched the subject. Best not to dwell on the negative aspects of the past. She was here to focus on the good things and emphasize the future. "Tell me, have you ever been to Florida, Bertie?"

The man's face cleared as he switched to a less fraught line of thought. "No, I don't think I ever have. Well, maybe for a day or two before a Caribbean cruise or some such thing. How did you end up living there?"

"That is a bit of a story. I met my husband in New York City and that is where we lived until he retired. He was in finance and needed to be where all the important stuff was happening. I loved it there. So much to do and see, and you just felt like it was the center of the universe; like *you* were at the center of the universe."

"Sounds wonderful, always fancied being at the center of the universe. Why did you leave?"

Annabelle sighed, "Something just changes when you retire. You don't get invited to everything like you once did. Many of the important people are younger and more beautiful. But…if you retire to Florida you can become the center of a slightly slower, less powerful, universe. So, we moved."

"Did you like it there?" Bertie looked intrigued by the idea.

"It was pleasant. Kind of like being on an everlasting cruise. Dinners, parties, nail appointments, shopping, charity committees, and, of course, for my husband it meant he could play golf almost every day. His idea of heaven." Her expression had turned solemn and she seemed to be looking far into the distance.

"I am sorry that you lost your husband. You must have loved him very much; you were married for a long time."

"I cared for him. We were good together. We were good together in New York, and we were content in Florida. We didn't have family to worry about. Regretfully, no children for either of us."

"I didn't think either you or I ever really were fond of children. We never talked about it much."

"No, but you can't help but wonder what you might have missed. I mean, simply everyone has them, after all." She paused and looked pointedly in the direction of the condensation-coated ice bucket.

Taking the cue, Bertie rose and opened the bottle with the perfect little pop and filled the flutes with a flourish.

When he handed her one, she smiled ruefully. "It made settling the estate easier to not have relatives clamoring for their bit of the pie."

"Yes, being an only child made my inheritance pretty straightforward."

Settled on the settee with their glasses they were quiet for some minutes, each thinking their own thoughts.

"Of course, there really isn't anyone to care about us or take care of us as we get older."

"True…"

"And that is why I came back to San Francisco. I may not have children but I have longtime friends, and we can take care of each other."

Bertie looked a little surprised. "I never thought of my friends taking care of me, or me taking care of them."

Annabelle would have bet on that but kept her opinion to herself. It was pretty obvious that Bertie didn't give thought to many things, and other people's needs would rank high on the list of things he didn't consider. She could tell she had piqued his interest as he rose to pour them a bit more bubbly.

CHAPTER TWENTY

The champagne was gone and the empty bottle rested, neck down, in the bucket of chilly water. Bertie was sufficiently buzzed and compliant, and now was the time for Annabelle to reveal why she was really here.

After her husband died, her therapist had asked her what the biggest risk she could take was. She'd thought about it for a few days and when she returned for her next appointment, she had her answer ready.

What she most deeply wanted, had maybe always wanted, was the life she'd left behind in San Francisco. She wanted another shot at her first marriage, she wanted to move into her rightful position in the city's social network. She wanted the respect of her old friends and the reclaiming of everything she had lost when she and Bertie broke up. She wanted the PU Club, the Bohemian Club ladies' nights and picnics. She wanted Bertie back and she wanted everything that bitch, Greta Gardner, had kept her from having.

It wasn't like Greta wanted it, she didn't even care. She'd never wanted Bertie, she just swanned through life taking whatever she fancied and left the weaklings, like Annabelle, in the dust. But Annabelle wasn't a weakling anymore. She would go back and reclaim her due.

The session with the therapist had been pretty intense and had climaxed with Annabelle declaring that Greta Gardner had better watch her back, because, when Annabelle was done, Greta wouldn't know what had hit her.

There'd still been fifteen minutes left in the session that was mostly spent with Dr. Caldicott trying to undo the damage he had wrought, but a genie released from the bottle was impossible to recapture. Annabelle didn't even really hear his pleas for calmness and forgiveness. She was too caught up with constructing her plan and thanked the shell-shocked man with effusive gratitude on her final exit from his office.

In making her preparations for the move back to San Francisco, Annabelle had plenty of time to think about her longtime friendship with Greta. In quieter moments Annabelle recognized that the real problem with Greta had been that she was so "nice." She was a person who took *noblesse oblige* to heart. Greta had welcomed both Annabelle and Bertie into her charmed circle, and once you were there it was required that you pay homage to her.

At some point Annabelle moved close to Bertie and rested her head on his shoulder. After a few moments he rested his head on her blond head. It was like muscle memory, this was how they had watched TV during their marriage, falling asleep, and then both waking with cricks in their necks.

"Remember this, Bertie? Remember how happy we were once?"

Bernie started a bit. He'd almost fallen asleep. "Yes...I do. What happened with us, anyway?"

"We should never have separated." She almost said "I should never have left you," but, that sounded so harsh, and she would have to admit responsibility and there was no way she could do that. She and Bertie were not responsible, it was all Greta's doing. But, she couldn't say that out loud, either. At least not yet.

She could tell that Bertie was dozing off again, so she sat up, causing him to jerk awake.

"It is getting quite late. What is it you wanted to talk to me about, Annabelle?"

"Bertie, I wanted to tell you that I have come back here to give us another chance. Don't look so worried. I'm not going to move in or anything, but I have a lot of money now and I know that some of your investments have not paid as they should."

"How would you know that? Who have you been talking to?"

"Bertie, I would never talk to anyone about your personal finances. I just understand business. But, this isn't about money, this is about us."

Bertie's boozy fog had cleared a bit and he looked a little concerned. "About us?"

"Don't look so worried. I just want to be part of your life, like the old friends that we are."

"Part of my life?" Bertie realized he was sounding dim, but all the wine and the late hour were not in his favor.

"Yes, just as friends. I want to see our old friends and have them get used to seeing us together."

"Together?"

"Yes, like at the PU Club for dinner, or Ladies' Night at the Bohemian Club. Isn't the Bohemian Grove picnic coming up this spring? Can you imagine everyone's faces when we show up together?"

Bertie did smile at that. He could completely imagine how they would be the center of attention if they arrived at the picnic together. It gave him quite a thrill to think of it. He hadn't been the center of attention like that in many years, and the idea excited him. "Yes, that would really knock their socks off, wouldn't it?"

Annabelle stood up abruptly. It was time to leave. She had planted the seed and there was no point in revealing her whole plan all at once. He was excited, but not alarmed, and there was no need to move too fast.

"I really must be heading home, dearest. I'll arrange an Uber and you can walk me downstairs."

Bertie stood too, though he was a little unsteady on his feet.

"I will just show myself to the powder room."

When she returned she found Bertie looking out at the lights of San Francisco with a slightly bemused look on his face. He turned to her. "You know, I find that I am rather delighted at the idea of seeing more of you, my dear."

"Me, too." She leaned into him and patted his chest. "My ride should be here in a couple of minutes. Walk me down, would you?"

"Of course."

It took only a few minutes for her car to show up and whisk her away to her apartment.

Bertie stood on the steps looking after the disappearing vehicle, slightly dazed, but pleasantly buoyed by the evening, then turned and went back into his lonely house. It already felt dimmer than he'd remembered it.

At her own home, Annabelle carefully performed the rites and rituals required to keep her sculpted, lifted, Botoxed, and tanned facade in perfect condition. The application of the serums and creams applied in the specific order and method had become a meditative ritual performed while her mind recited her mantra of vindication.

Tonight, had been the perfect start. She would begin the process of reacquainting herself and ingratiating herself with their circle. Joining the fund-raising committees for the museums, galleries, ballet, opera, and symphony. She would be seen with Bertie in public and before long she would be the one invited to the dinner parties as his partner. Those hopeful ladies who had made up the numbers in the past would be dropped by the wayside or coupled with less desirable partners. Oh, and Bertie, who had not been all that sought-after, would become much more visible. Her generous donations, elaborate arrangements, and helpful suggestions would elevate them to the couple everyone would want included in their event. She made a slight face. Well, everyone over a certain age. They would never be the golden young couple, but they could still have their moment, and if she worked it right, by summer she'd be having the "go to" party of the season in her new home on Walnut Street.

CHAPTER TWENTY-ONE

Kestrel had taken a string bag and her wallet when she went to the farmer's market that morning. She stopped at TJ's on the way home and didn't want the extra baggage of phones and all the other crap she usually carried around in her dingy gym bag. As it was she could hardly make it up that last hill from the bus stop with the bundles of veggies doomed to die a terrible death in the back of her fridge, along with the delights of a cruise through Trader Joe's including the final addition, after much debate, of a container of dark chocolate peanut butter cups.

She probably should not have included the two bottles of cheap wine that added incredible weight to her burdens, but it was too late now. On previous shopping trips she had improved the day of some local miscreant by leaving bottles of unopened wine at the bus stop when they became too heavy. Sometimes she donated to a likely-looking denizen of the San Francisco streets, but she'd been known to just leave it sitting there, waiting for the next unsuspecting passerby.

When she finally reached her front door she was startled to find it standing ajar. WTF, her heart leapt. She knew she didn't leave it unlocked, much less standing open when she left. Then she spotted the bashed section of the window in the door, hung with faded IKEA curtains, and the spattering of glass just inside.

"Shit!" She pushed the door the rest of the way open with her shoulder and heaved the heavy bags onto the counter. Oh yeah, someone unfriendly had been here all right. The cabinets and drawers hung open. OMG, she ran for the bedroom. She'd hoped that anyone with any experience would have passed up the crappy-looking duffel sitting next to the bed, but no, this idiot had been an amateur and took the bulky bag with him.

"My phone! My God, my phone is gone." She tried to calm herself before going into complete panic mode. In fact, both phones were gone, but only one of them mattered. The one with the texts and messages from her mother and the cat videos didn't matter, but the one with the secret lives of half the damned city and all her contacts was gone, as well.

She had to take several deep breaths to bring herself to the point of figuring out what to do next. First, the phone was locked, and openable only with her code or her fingerprint. Okay, breathe a little slower now. Then, she thought she could probably contact the service provider and stop the service. Then what? OMG, I don't know. Can I get my stuff back? Damn, I just paid $1200 for the newest iPhone. Did the renters insurance cover this; and the $500 Gucci sunglasses, and the $800 Laboutin heels?

Breathe. First call the service provider and stop the service. The thief would probably just wipe the phone and sell it as quickly as possible, but maybe it was someone who knew that she was *SFUndertheRug.com*. That's stupid. Just relax.

She darted outside to open the garage door. For some crazy reason this thief had not thought to go into the garage and that's where her laptop still sat from her last visit to the coffee shop.

What was on the damned phone, anyway? Only everything! All the phone numbers, the e-mails the photos, the posts…everything.

Who would have broken in here, and why? Was it random, was it targeted? Did they break into Sam's place as well? She knew that calling the police was pointless. They'd come out, spread fingerprint powder all over the place, take a report, and disappear. Would she ever even hear back from them? She'd be better off haunting the local flea markets or checking Craigslist for postings.

Carrying the laptop Kestrel darted to Sam's side of the duplex. The door was locked but she grabbed his key from the cute brass elephant key rack behind her door and fitted it into the lock. It opened and she entered. She hadn't thought to knock but it didn't look like he was home. It also didn't look like anyone had been rummaging through his stuff, although it was difficult to tell. The piles of books on the floor and file folders on the table and chairs did not look disturbed, but who would steal that crap anyway? It didn't look like anyone had rifled through cabinets or underwear drawers so she relocked the door and returned to her place.

It seemed to take forever to contact the provider and tell them to lock the phone. She told them she'd be there in twenty minutes to get a new phone and see what could be rescued from the cloud.

Three deep breaths, that's what her grandmother always told her to take, but at the end of it she was worse off than before. Not only was her phone gone, but she felt lightheaded from all that deep breathing.

Everything that could be done was done. Kestrel had acquired a new iPhone from her provider, had canceled access to her old phone, downloaded her info and contacts to the new phone, and could only hope that the asshole who had stolen her phone had been content with the few measly dollars he could get for used electronics.

The first person she called when everything had been straightened out was not her cop former boyfriend but her slightly sketchy actor/private detective friend, Lester. The call went straight to voicemail. "Lester, it's Kestrel. Call me back, my apartment got robbed while I was out and I need some security advice."

It didn't take long for him to call back. She picked up right away when the phone rang. "Lester, thanks for calling."

"No problem, K, I was on the phone with my agent."

Kestrel didn't want to spend the time talking about it, but figured it was only polite to ask any actor what he was talking to his agent about. "That's good. Got some new irons in the fire?"

"Yeah, a couple of auditions this week, but Hollywood isn't beating down my door. In the meantime, I can come check out your place and see what kind of security system would be best. You may only need an interactive doorbell."

"What is that? Crooks don't usually ring the bell, do they?"

"The device just notifies you when anyone comes to the door."

"Notifies me?"

"Yeah, just pings your phone and you can see what is going on. You'll probably need better locks, as well. Doesn't do you a lot of good to watch some random dude break in."

"Well, in this case, they just broke the window and let themselves in. Besides, my phones were part of what was stolen."

"Okay, well, I can't get there today, but I will let you know when I can come. In the meantime, just get your window fixed."

"No shit, Sherlock."

CHAPTER TWENTY-TWO

After Kestrel had finished her lunch shift at The Towers it took two buses, and a mile of walking to get to the house on Walnut Street.

She'd never been to this house before but imagined that many of the people in the neighborhood would find her very familiar-looking if they glanced out their window and observed her progress up the street. They wouldn't know where they knew her from, but they would realize they knew her from somewhere. A clue might be if they suddenly got the urge to order food or another glass of wine, but they would shrug it off and just wonder what she was doing in their neighborhood.

Much of the discussion at last night's gig at the PU Club and this morning at The Towers had swirled around the death of Greta Gardner over the previous weekend. Of course, she'd been ill for some time, so her dying wasn't too much of a shock. But the fact that the police had indicated that it was a suspicious death made it an even more scintillating topic. The morning paper had been pretty scant on the details, but

Kestrel's cell phone had been blowing up with messages from Beatrice. She had called Kestrel on Sunday evening after the police had completed questioning her and was panicked. They had not arrested her, but she seemed to be a possible suspect. She lived in the house and had found the body. She was still in Greta's house because she didn't have a separate residence and she had no place else to go. The police had told her not to leave town. Why would she leave town? Why had they told her that? Did they think she drowned Greta in her bathtub?

Kestrel had promised to come to Beatrice after she got off work, and here she was trudging up Walnut Street. Beatrice had told her to call when she got there. The main part of the house was a crime scene and only her quarters, off the back of the garage, were open.

Kestrel called and a few moments later the garage door slowly slid up. She thought that she had become more interesting to any observers since she was entering the Gardner house through the garage. She glanced around the neighborhood but saw no one. Maybe she was only imagining the neighbors and their staff standing back peering at her from the windows above.

Beatrice was not looking good. Usually, her dark skin glowed and she was a person that inspired confidence and comfort. Today she seemed older and stooped from her usually regal stance.

She hurried Kestrel into the pristine garage and quickly slid the door closed. She also felt as if she were being observed by the neighbors.

"Come through here. My quarters are here in the back of the garage." Actually, Kestrel was surprised to see that the "servant's quarters" where Beatrice stayed were nicer than the apartments of most of the people she knew. The rooms were reached through the garage but opened out onto that miracle of miracles in San Francisco, a sunny open garden with a patch of lawn, a patio, and flowerbeds. In the temperate climate she could see a bed of Cymbidium and Phalaenopsis orchids sheltered under a small gazebo. She'd been told they thrived in this climate, but she'd managed to kill off all of hers when she'd tried to grow them.

Beatrice had a small sitting room, a bedroom, and her own bathroom. There was no kitchen, but she had full access to the kitchen in the main house.

It was afternoon and Kestrel saw the remains of Beatrice's lunch on the side table. Half a nibbled sandwich and a long-cold cup of coffee. There was a small collection of liquor bottles on the table, as well, and a glass that looked to contain Beatrice's favorite drink, a Dark 'n' Stormy:

dark rum and ginger beer.

"It is so terrible being here. I don't think I should be here with Greta gone, but I have no place else to go. Most of the house is taped off and the police were here all yesterday searching through everything. They had a warrant for my rooms, but of course, I have nothing they can't see. But it is too terrible to have strangers digging through everything. Your papers and your underwear. Your dirty clothes hamper!"

"Yes, I know, Beatrice. They searched my place a couple of years ago. It felt so intrusive. Tell me what's been happening today?"

"I don't really know. They asked a lot more questions, about my alibi…I never ever thought in my life I would have one of those. An alibi!"

"All of that is completely normal. They have to know where everyone was so they know who doesn't have an alibi. It's fine, I'm sure. Nobody could ever think you would kill someone."

Kestrel sounded more confident than she was. Who knows what the police might think? "Did they tell you anything?"

"No, that Inspector Burns is very nice, but he tells me nothing."

"Bobby Burns? Oh, great."

"What? What is wrong with Inspector Burns?" Beatrice looked alarmed.

"There's nothing wrong with him. He's the best you could have on the case."

Beatrice looked a little comforted by that.

"You don't have to stay here, do you? You could go stay someplace else if you wanted, right?"

"Yes, but I have no place. The only other place I have lived is with the Spencers and I can't go there. Oh, my dear, Mrs. Spencer will never let me see the girls again, after this." Her voice had begun to rise in pitch again.

"It is okay, Beatrice. I am just thinking that it must be extremely uncomfortable for you to stay here. I think you should pack a bag and come stay with me. I only have one bedroom and you'll have to sleep on the couch, but I am gone a lot at work and I'm a pretty good roommate."

Beatrice threw her arms around Kestrel. "Oh, thank you. It is so terrible being here, especially if someone did kill Greta."

"It's okay, just pack a bag for tonight. I have a day off tomorrow and we'll come back with the car and get the rest of your things."

Beatrice went into the bedroom and packed quickly. It was amazing how fast she could move when motivated.

When they were ready to go Kestrel realized there was just one thing more to do. "You'd better send a text to Inspector Burns. Just tell him you are staying with Kestrel Jonas for a few days. He already knows the address."

Bobby was not going to be happy that his prime suspect was staying with his ex-girlfriend, but what could she say? You gotta do what you gotta do.

CHAPTER TWENTY-THREE

When Kestrel and Beatrice reached her place, Sam's side of the duplex was dark, so the introductions would have to wait until the next day. Sam could be a pain in the ass but he had saved her behind more than once. It could be useful to have an attorney as a neighbor, especially one who thought of you as his goofy little sister and was willing to give free legal advice to you and your friends.

Of course, the first thing Kestrel did was open a bottle of wine. Unfortunately, they hadn't thought to bring Beatrice's dark rum and ginger beer with them when they packed up her things. So, she poured each of them a glass of wine. Since she had come into a bit more money in the past year, she didn't depend on cheap wine from TJ's to stock her cabinet anymore. Her taste hadn't improved that much, but she did actually shop at Whole Paycheck once in a while. It seemed there should be some benefit from inheriting part of her deadbeat dad's estate. A simple DNA test had linked her to one of San Francisco's wealthiest families and embroiled her in a murder investigation.

Kestrel let Beatrice lead the conversation. First she assured her that nothing she told Kestrel would be making its way onto the hyperspace pages of her blog, *SFUndertheRug.com*. That was how they knew each other. Beatrice was one of the cadre of service staff in San Francisco who often shared their world and the doings of their employers with her. Sometimes for fun, sometimes for a little extra cash, and sometimes out of spite and revenge. Beatrice wasn't that kind of contact. They'd met not long after Beatrice moved to San Francisco and went to work for the Spencer family as a nanny. Until their ugly divorce that shook up Beatrice's world, she'd never talked about them, but she thought the rarefied attitudes and arrogance of the Spencers' wealthy friends was both appalling and hysterical, and so she shared stories with Kestrel, both of them having a few drinks and laughing their heads off. It didn't surprise Kestrel so much that people wanted to read about the antics of the elite, but that the elite performed so many antics. Sometimes it was like a high-end version of *Jerry Springer*, on steroids.

When she noticed that Beatrice was falling asleep in her chair, Kestrel roused herself to go into her bedroom so her friend could get some sleep. She had the wherewithal to find a decent pillow and case, sheet, and blanket, so they weren't completely doing the couch surfing thing, and then she grabbed the wine bottle and headed for her own bed.

Settled into her extra-large, overstretched Grateful Dead shirt from the 1970s and a pair of sweatpants she threw the window open wide, turned off the light, poured the last of the wine into her glass and climbed into her bed. It was cool outside; pretty much all San Francisco nights were cool, even in what you might call the heat of summer, which was rarely ever hot. She loved the air, heavy with the ocean dampness that slipped through the window and seemed to sink to the floor and curl around the room. She sat in the bed with her knees up and leaned forward to look out into the night sky. San Francisco, the place that Herb Caen had called Baghdad by the Bay. What a strange and magical city. Full of all the joys and terrors of any city, but with a twist. She realized her wayward thoughts were probably more a result of too much wine than her love for her surroundings. The past few months, okay, maybe the past couple of years, she had realized that she was drinking a lot of wine, as in *a lot* of wine. She didn't think of that as necessarily a bad thing, or a good thing, but an unexpected, possibly unnecessary thing. Since she'd found, then lost, her sister Grace, wine seemed to be the natural accompaniment to whatever was happening in her day. Stressed? Have a glass of wine. Celebrating? More wine. Tired, wired, whatever, wine was the answer. It made her feel better. Or maybe, it just made her feel something or stop feeling something. Oh, well. She drained the glass and lay back on the bed. She'd think about it tomorrow, unless she was stressed, happy, celebrating, tired, or anything else, then maybe she'd think about it the day after that.

Tomorrow was a rare day off from both of her jobs and she fell asleep making her plans. First she'd get the old VW out of the garage and take Beatrice back to Walnut Street to pick up more of her stuff. She'd get Beatrice and Sam together so they could walk through everything that had happened with Greta and see if they could make sense of it and figure out what the police were thinking. She might get in touch with Bobby Burns and see if he could give her any information, though she was pretty sure he would not be willing to do that. If she could just find out what they thought had happened in that house while Beatrice was away, that would help so much. They'd be checking Beatrice's alibi, and they'd be following up on people who usually came by the house. She'd see if she could get Bobby to talk to her in the morning.

As it was, she didn't have to make a plan for talking to Bobby. Promptly at nine a.m. the next day there came a knock at the door. Who the heck would be knocking on her door at nine a.m.? Certainly not anyone who knew her.

She staggered out of her bedroom and through the darkened living room, trying not to wake Beatrice and hoping to get to the door before the racket started up again. She flung the door open just as Bobby Burns was raising his fist to knock again.

"Bobby, shhh...people are trying to sleep. What are you doing here?" she hissed.

"I'm trying to find out how you are involved in my murder investigation." Bobby lowered his voice but he still sounded agitated.

Kestrel glanced over her shoulder toward her sleeping guest and stepped out onto the porch, pulling the door closed behind her. "I'm not involved in your murder investigation. I'm just letting a friend stay here for a few days. She didn't want to stay in that creepy house where her friend died and she didn't have any place else to go."

Bobby eyed her skeptically. "You're not messing around trying to figure things out?"

"Of course not." Kestrel lied straight to his face.

"Sam's not involved in this or working on it?"

"I told you, no." Of course, she didn't mention that she just hadn't had a chance to involve Sam yet. It was good that he hadn't been home last night so she didn't have to fib any more than necessary.

Bobby seemed to relax a bit. "Okay, then. It just seemed odd that out of all the people in San Francisco, you'd be the one coming to Ms. Campbell's rescue."

"I've known Beatrice for years… she helps me with my blog sometimes."

"Ah…"

"What does that mean?"

"Nothing. Just, ah. So, she's one of your army of mystery minions?"

"I don't have an army of minions, mystery or otherwise. Beatrice is a friend who happens to work for and around the people I write about. She's a good person and she needed someone to help her until this gets straightened out."

"I just don't want you to get involved.…"

"Involved in what? Besides, it is none of your business what I get involved in, Bobby."

"I know, you just seem to have a habit of getting mixed up in things."

"It's not my fault that I am inquisitive and pay attention to what's going on around me, is it?"

"I don't know…maybe."

That made Kestrel laugh and even Bobby cracked a smile. Maybe he was being ridiculous, he thought. It wasn't really that farfetched that Kestrel and Beatrice Campbell would know one another.

CHAPTER TWENTY-FOUR

"Do you want a cup of coffee? I'm dying for some. Go around to the back deck and I'll make some and bring it out. Beatrice is asleep on the couch. We were up kind of late last night."

Kestrel went back into the kitchen and quickly made a fresh pot of coffee. There was half a pot of stale brew from yesterday that she'd normally have just zapped in the microwave, but she thought better about serving it to a guest. Bobby wasn't much of a guest. They'd shared hundreds of pots of coffee and lots of other things in the past, but it just seemed more civilized to make fresh coffee. Hell, when had life become so complicated?

While the coffee brewed she went to the bedroom to put on some slippers and a sweater and then carried the two cups of coffee out the door and around to the deck where Bobby waited.

"It's beautiful and sunny out here this morning. Are these the same dead plants that were here before or are they new?"

"They are new, and they are not completely dead, smart ass. Here's your coffee."

It felt comfortable to be amiably arguing with Bobby again. She sure had her stock of big brothers to take care of her. She wondered if she'd ever meet someone who didn't think of her as a little sister, though. "So, how is Rocky doing in her new job? She's in fraud now, right?"

"She's doing good. Picked up a new case where someone is scamming people in San Francisco."

"Whoa, big surprise."

"I know, right? How about you? How's it going with the new family?"

"Pretty much the way it was going before they knew I existed. I heard from them, or their attorney, a lot more before they had to admit we had the same dad. I don't really see the Graham family at the PU Club much, anymore." She wondered about that for a moment. "Maybe someone at the club lets them know when I'm not working."

"George Musgrove's trial is still kicking around the courts. Not even sure he'll ever be charged for anything substantial. He may have intended to kill her, but he really only stole her computer and phone after she was dead."

"And the family got the money back that Garrett Jr. had given him."

They sat companionably for several minutes, enjoying the tepid warmth of the sunshine. Finally, Kestrel spoke. "You know, I had Thanksgiving with Grace's family in Menlo Park."

"Really, how was that?"

"It was strange, but it was okay. They're nice people and they want to be friendly, but I think me looking so much like Grace makes them uncomfortable. It makes them sad and I can't really blame them. I wonder if they wish I was the one who'd died."

"Of course, they don't."

"They might. Sometimes that is what I think…no, wait. Don't get all protective of my feelings. I'm just saying that they must wonder how these things happen sometimes. Who goes and who stays."

Again, there was silence.

The glass door to the apartment slid open and Beatrice stuck her head out. "Good morning… I thought I heard someone talking out here." She stopped abruptly and her smile faded when she spotted Bobby.

"Hey, Beatrice. Inspector Burns and I are old friends and he just stopped by to see how you were doing."

"Uh, thanks, I guess. Is that coffee?"

"Yep, the rest of the pot is in the kitchen. Why don't you get a cup and join us?" Kestrel stood up and grabbed one of the folding chairs leaning against the outside wall for Beatrice. Three chairs, the tiny table, and the various half-dead potted plants took almost every inch of space on the tiny deck.

When Beatrice had joined them Bobby finally spoke. "Ms. Campbell, when I got your message that you were staying here I did want to make sure you were doing okay, but I also have some additional questions for you. Can we talk now?"

"I guess so, you're already here."

Kestrel stood again. "I can go inside so you have privacy."

Beatrice grabbed onto her hand, "No, don't go in. It's okay if she's here isn't it?" she said to Bobby.

"It is all right with me if you want Ms. Jonas to be here. But she is not really a part of the discussion so she should probably refrain from interrupting."

"In other words, keep my big trap shut." Kestrel laughed and Beatrice smiled.

"Well, to be blunt..." Bobby laughed. "I wanted to let you know that your alibi checks out. You were known to be at the Spencers' home that night before the children went to bed and to depart from there Sunday morning. That is not to say that you couldn't have left during the night, but we are checking their security camera system to confirm activity at the home."

"Nice," Beatrice grimaced. "Mrs. Spencer will never let me see the girls again after the police have been there."

"Since you were not with Ms. Gardner on Saturday night you can't tell us whether anyone else came to the house to see her. But, you can give us a list of people she might have been expecting or who came to see here while you've been living there."

"Not a lot of people came. I mean she had a lot of friends, and when I was first working for her they would come by and she would go out with them, but when she started feeling sicker most of them stopped coming over. They would call her, of course. Did you check her phone for calls? Most people would call before they came over."

"We are checking her phone and there were a couple of calls that day that we are following up on. But, who specifically, would come to see her?"

"Mr. Frankel came by pretty often. Mostly when he was on his way to dinner with friends. He'd come by on his way and gossip for a bit. He could have come by on Saturday."

"Has there been anybody unusual, anybody that doesn't usually visit?"

"Just that one old friend of hers from Florida. She only came once, a couple of weeks ago. I remember her name because it was unusual, kind of sing-songy. Ms. Annabelle Leigh, she said."

"You wouldn't have a number for her would you?"

"Oh, no. I only ever saw her the one time."

"Anyone else?"

"I don't think so, except for a few weeks ago. I stayed with the girls on a Saturday night, but I hadn't planned it in advance so I stopped by the house in the afternoon to pick up my toothbrush and all and let Greta know I would be gone until morning."

"Who was there then?"

"Well, I didn't see anybody there. It's just that Ms. Gardner acted kind of flustered and there was a champagne bottle and two glasses downstairs in the living room and a briefcase I had never seen before. Greta said Bertie, Mr. Frankel, had been there. I figured he'd left his briefcase and would come back for it. I never saw him with a briefcase before, any of the times he visited."

"Was the briefcase still there when you returned the next morning?"

"No, I never saw it again after that afternoon."

"Did you usually take Ms. Gardner out shopping or for appointments?"

"I drove her to her appointments, but I usually did the household shopping myself. Mostly they were doctor appointments. Last week I took her to her attorney's office."

"Do you know the attorney's name?"

"I don't recall his name. I might never have heard it. I just drove her to the building on Van Ness, made sure she got upstairs, and waited in the car for her. She called me when she was finished."

"I guess that is about it. Just one more thing, do you know if there is a safe in Ms. Gardner's home?"

"Yes, there is a safe in her bedroom, in the back of the standing wardrobe. The one with the old-fashioned painted doors."

"Do you know the combination of the safe?"

"No, sir. I have no idea."

"All right then." Bobby stood up and turned to Kestrel. "Thanks for the coffee." He turned back to Beatrice. "Be sure to let us know if you change residence. Ms. Gardner's home is a sealed crime scene, but you still have access to your rooms downstairs."

When she was sure he was gone Beatrice slumped in her chair. Her usual ramrod posture just crumpled. "Being questioned by the police is so frightening. I feel like I am lying when I am not."

"Bobby makes everybody feel like that."

"How do you know Inspector Burns…Bobby?"

"I met him when I had some business with the police a couple of years ago and we kind of dated for a while. Let's go in and get some breakfast and get dressed. I have someone I want you to meet, and then we will go get the rest of your stuff."

Kestrel was able to wrangle up a couple of bowls of slightly stale Captain Crunch and the last of a quart of not-quite-turned milk for their breakfast. "Sorry about the cereal, I'm fresh out of Pop-Tarts and haven't had a chance to get to the store."

"Don't worry about me, I spent most of the last few years taking care of children. I am familiar with all versions of cold cereals, except for the healthier ones. I am partial to Lucky Charms, myself."

"Me, too."

CHAPTER TWENTY-FIVE

When they were fed and dressed Beatrice followed Kestrel out the door and almost walked into her when she took an immediate left and knocked on the door three feet from her own.

If the big, sleepy man who answered the knock was surprised to be greeted by Kestrel and her smiling, but slightly confused friend, he didn't show it. He just grunted, turned, and shuffled back into his apartment with them trailing along behind him.

"Sorry to wake you up, Sam, I wasn't sure if you'd be home or if you were going into the office today." Kestrel went to the sink and filled the coffee carafe with water. It was obvious she knew her way around his coffee maker.

"I'll be going in later. We worked most of the weekend so I was sleeping in."

"I'm making us all some coffee. We need to talk to you." As she spooned ground coffee into the coffeemaker, she waved her hand in Beatrice's direction. "This is my friend Beatrice. Beatrice, this is my neighbor, Sam."

Sam only grunted and closed the bedroom door behind himself.

"I don't think your friend is very happy to see us. Maybe we should come back another time," worried Beatrice.

"He's always like that in the morning, and we need to talk to him before he starts working and gets sucked into all that legal crap he does."

"What kind of legal crap? Is he a policeman, too?"

"No, he's an attorney, I thought I told you."

"I don't think I need an attorney. You don't think I need an attorney, do you?" Beatrice sounded alarmed.

"No, I don't think you need an attorney, and if you did, it wouldn't be Sam, it would be someone from the public defender's office. Sam just knows a lot of stuff about the law and I want him to hear what's going on and tell us what he thinks."

By the time Sam exited the bedroom he had washed his grumpy face, shaved, and changed into an inexpensive and ill-fitting business suit. His hair was mostly combed and his limp shirt was mostly tucked into his trousers. However, he was smiling, and much less forbidding than he had been a few minutes earlier. The coffee was ready and Kestrel had filled his favorite mug, the one that said WORLD'S GREATEST LAWYER (the one she'd bought him when she didn't have to go to jail) and doctored it up with a hefty dollop of half-and-half and three heaping spoons of sugar, just as he liked it.

"Nice to meet you, Beatrice. Come on in and sit down." He turned back to the dining table and only then realized that, as usual, there was only one chair that was not piled with books and papers. "Um, just move the stuff on to the floor and have a seat."

Kestrel helped Beatrice clear a chair, cleared one for herself, and brought each of them a cup of fresh coffee from the kitchen. "Beatrice needs help. Not really help, just some advice. Her employer may have been murdered and she found the body and she, we, are worried that the police might think she did it."

"Wow, that's quite a morning wake-up." Sam looked a little taken aback. He turned to Beatrice. "Why don't you just tell me what happened from the beginning…and Kestrel will just listen and fill in the blanks later."

Kestrel slumped back in her chair, "Wow, I think we have a theme going here."

It took Beatrice about half an hour and more coffee all around to fill Sam in on her relationship with Greta Gardner and the events of the past few weeks.

When she was done Sam was silent for a couple of minutes, then, sat back in his chair. "You said that Ms. Gardner was doing better and that she was in a medical study. Had she said anything to you about that lately?"

"Yes, she did tell me that the man from the cancer center, his name is Sandy, or something like that, called and told her that her last test results and scans looked really good. I was so happy for her, we talked about doing something to celebrate the good news."

Sam had been taking some notes and looked them over, scribbling a couple more comments at the bottom of the page. "I can see why you would be worried about the police. You are the first on the list of suspects just because you lived there. You found the body and your fingerprints are no doubt everywhere. They will be trying to figure out if the two of you got along, if you were mad at her, like maybe if she fired you because she was getting better. They'll try to determine if you stand to benefit from her death in any way or if you have something to hide."

Beatrice looked away from him uncomfortably when he made the last statement. "I can see that you are probably right."

"Yes, but they won't just try to pin this on you. They'll try to eliminate you as a suspect and move on to the next possible person. It's a complex process. Have you talked to them? Have they told you the cause of death or asked any other questions?"

"Yes, Inspector Burns was here this morning. He said they were still checking my alibi because I could have left the Spencer home during the night. They asked about other people that had been to see Greta in the past few weeks."

"Great...Bobby Burns." Sam and Kestrel glanced at each other; Kestrel shrugged. "Did they tell you to stay in town?"

"Yes, and they said to let them know where I was if I moved from here."

"From here?"

Kestrel finally spoke. "She's staying with me for a while. Staying in the house was creepy and she didn't have anywhere else to go. We are going to go pick up some of her stuff. Do you want to come along?"

"No thanks, Bobby already doesn't like me much. Besides, I am going in late today, but I do have to go to the office."

Since they were already dressed and sufficiently caffeinated, Kestrel and Beatrice chugged the old VW Bug out of the garage and headed for the Gardner home.

"How come you tell me you never meet any good-looking men, Kestrel? We've talked with two just this morning."

"Yeah, they are both damned cute in their own way, but they just think of me as a goofball. More like the Rosalind Russell type in *His Girl Friday*. A pal…"

Beatrice thought about that for a minute. "If you say so, but I think it is you that thinks you aren't the romantic lead in this comedy. Don't forget, I perfected my English watching old movies. You could still end up with one of them, in the end."

"Nah, I'm still waiting for the bad boy to come along, like Marlon Brando in, well, in almost anything." They both laughed.

CHAPTER TWENTY-SIX

Beatrice had taken the garage door opener away with her the night before so they pulled into the driveway as the door slid open.

Beatrice went into her quarters to begin packing and Kestrel pulled the sleeve of her sweatshirt down over her hand and tried the door to the kitchen. It was locked. "Hey, Beatrice. Do you have a key to this door, and a pair of gloves?"

Beatrice came out of the bedroom. "Yes, I have keys to all of the doors in the house. I thought Inspector Burns said the house was off limits."

"He did, but there's nobody here and I'm not going to touch anything." They stared each other down for several seconds before Beatrice sighed and plucked a key off the row of hooks on the wall inside her door, handing it to Kestrel. "There are some disposable gloves in that drawer," she said motioning toward a cabinet in the garage. "I'll be in my room not paying any attention to what you are doing that you shouldn't be."

Kestrel opened the top drawer of the cabinet and found a box of nitrile gloves, purple, no less. She pulled them on and carefully unlocked the door to the house, slipping the key into her pocket. She took her shoes off so that she wouldn't be making any mess, or noise, or leaving any traces.

It was interesting to see how the very rich lived. She'd heard many tales of older members of the upper crust in San Francisco moldering away in their mansions on the hill. They had inherited these great old homes from Mummy and Daddy, and it was cheaper just to stay in them but it cost a lot to keep them up. This one wasn't exactly Miss Havisham material, but it could have used some upgrading.

Kestrel was careful not to touch anything, just walking around the rooms looking for anything interesting. As usual, everything was currently dusted with fingerprint dust. Once when her house had been robbed she'd been appalled at the mess the police left when looking for clues. Somehow she'd thought they would clean up after themselves, especially since they basically concluded that there was no way in hell that she'd ever see her VCR again. But, no, not so much. Certainly, Greta Gardner wouldn't be complaining about the mess.

Eventually she found herself at the bottom of the stairs looking up toward the "scene of the crime." She heard Beatrice's voice from the garage. "I'm going to be ready to go in about five minutes. Don't touch anything." Why were her friends all so bossy to her? She couldn't imagine.

She climbed the stairs, careful not to touch the banisters, covered in powdery residue. She didn't want to be smearing stuff or messing up the scene. There was only one door open on the top landing, probably the only room she'd need to look at.

She bumped the door farther open with her elbow and tiptoed into the room. Knowing Beatrice, she was pretty sure this was not how the room usually looked. Everything had been opened and rifled through and the bed lay unmade, the sheets removed.

She moved on to the bathroom where Beatrice had found Greta's body. Peering from the doorway she found there wasn't much to see. All the bottles and candles Beatrice had described had been removed and the medicine cabinet stood open and empty. Kestrel was just imagining Beatrice finding her friend drowned in the bathtub when a click and bumping noise made her jump. It sounded like someone had come up behind her but, spinning around, she saw no one. Then she felt a nudge and looked down to find an insistent little vacuuming device edging its way around her feet in its constant quest for dirt. She breathed a sigh of relief and stepped out of the way of the little worker.

Beatrice called from the bottom of the stairs. "Come down, Kestrel. I'm ready to go and we need to get out of here. How are we going to explain being in here if someone comes?"

"Okay, okay, I'm coming." Kestrel moved quickly from the room and down the stairs. "Dang, that little vacuum thing scared the shit out of me. Does it just go around the house all the time?"

Beatrice was already headed for the garage and spoke over her shoulder, "No, there are two of them, one upstairs and one downstairs. They're on timers and on alternate days they turn on, vacuum their level, and then just go into their little houses and turn off again."

"Wait, what little houses?" Kestrel halted Beatrice's progress by grabbing her arm.

"Over there, under the desk. That one is 'Dobby, the house elf' and the one upstairs is 'Hazel the maid.'"

"Funny. I guess I'd name mine if I had one, too." For a moment she considered getting one. Housework was not her strong suit.

"Kestrel, can we please go? I don't like being here, and if you think every single house on this block is not watching to see what we are doing, you are crazy."

"You're right. Let's get out of here."

Beatrice had already piled her stuff in the front-end trunk of the VW and in the backseat and as they opened the garage door and backed out of the driveway, three conveniently situated dog walkers, only two with dogs, just happened to be strolling, slowly, past the house.

Kestrel drove just far enough away to be out of sight of any observers and then pulled over to the curb. She pulled out her phone and speed-dialed Bobby Burns. She was actually relieved when the call went to voicemail and she was able to leave a message about the robot vacuums in case the police hadn't thought to check them out. The little suckers could have picked up any little clues before the police ever got to the scene. She was just glad she didn't have to explain how she knew that they operated in the Walnut Street house, though she'd definitely have lied if he'd asked.

CHAPTER TWENTY-SEVEN

It took them a little longer to get home as the main gas tank of the VW ran dry, rolling down Lombard Street. They were on a downhill slope so they were able to coast along for a few moments while Kestrel reached down and switched to the one-gallon emergency tank. She immediately began the search for a filling station, not always an easy thing to find in that neighborhood. She'd once made the mistake of forgetting that she'd made the switch and found herself stranded on the side of the highway with nary a drop of gas.

As she pulled into her driveway she spotted Lester Stuyvesant just walking away from her door. "Damn, I forgot I was supposed to meet Lester today." She rolled into the driveway and cranked down her window. "Lester, I'm so sorry. There's been a lot of stuff going on and I forgot we were going to meet. I hope I'm not too late."

"No, that's fine. Slow day for me, anyway." Lester barely needed to lean down to peer across Kestrel toward Beatrice. He was not a tall person and since he'd given up his heeled boots and taken to wearing more leather vests and longer hair in homage to Tyrion Lannister, he appeared even shorter than he'd seemed before. It was a switch for him that he'd gone from bemoaning his short stature to almost wishing he actually could be considered a "little person." Unfortunately, he was a tad over five feet tall, so he didn't quite qualify. "Who's the lovely lady riding with you today, Kestrel? I see you've been holding out on me."

"Always the smooth one with the ladies, Lester. This is my friend Beatrice. Beatrice, this is Lester. *Bon vivant*, aspiring actor, and private investigator extraordinaire."

Beatrice smiled and reached across Kestrel to take Lester's outstretched hand. "Nice to meet you, Lester." As Lester stepped back and opened Kestrel's door Beatrice turned to her. "That's three good-looking men today."

Lester helped the two women haul Beatrice's belongings into the duplex and pile them in the corner of the living room. "It's going to be pretty crowded in here for the two of you."

"It won't be for long, I hope." Suddenly Beatrice sat down on the couch that had become her bed. "Damn, I just realized I'm going to have to find a job and a place to live pretty quick. And, I kind of think I won't be getting a reference from Greta." Then she burst into tears.

Lester looked kind of uncomfortable and glanced back and forth between Kestrel and the crying Beatrice a couple of times before clearing his throat.

"Um, I don't have a job for you, but I do have an extra bedroom in my apartment that I've been trying to rent out. I wasn't really thinking it could be a lady, but there's no reason it couldn't be, I guess. I mean, I'm kind of messy and keep weird hours, but I'm quiet, and not much of a threat." It was obvious he felt like he was going out on a limb making the offer. It was like asking someone out on a date. If they got all embarrassed and tried to come up with an excuse then everyone was uncomfortable. That was the main reason Lester seldom asked anyone out on a date, that and being the shortest guy in almost any room.

Beatrice smiled at him through her tears. "You know, I'm the one that is a murder suspect, so you might be more worried about whether or not I am a threat."

"I could get a lock for my bedroom door, or for yours, as well."

It surprised Kestrel when Beatrice said thoughtfully, "You know. I will really consider it when the dust settles here. If they don't put me in jail, I will need a place to go while I look for work. And, believe me, I promise you are not as messy as two six-year-olds."

Kestrel needed to talk to Lester about improving the security of her duplex, so they retired to the kitchen table to talk while Beatrice unpacked some of her toiletries and clothes, tucking them into open space in the living and bathroom, not that there was much of that available. It was not a big place. "Kestrel, do you mind if I take a shower?" she called out.

"Not at all, there are clean towels in the linen closet in the hallway. I have cheap shampoo, conditioner, and shower gel."

"No problem, I have my own." Beatrice opened the linen closet door and surveyed the jumbled contents. After a moment she took a chance and pulled a terrycloth item from the middle of a pile. Huh, lucky the first time she thought. "You know, I learned a trick for folding fitted sheets from a video online."

Not taking offense, Kestrel just laughed. "That's what we can do to entertain ourselves after dinner." And turned back to Lester.

Once the bathroom door had closed and they could hear the shower running Lester looked up from the information he'd brought. "So, what is up with Beatrice? What's this about being a murder suspect?"

Kestrel quickly brought Lester up to date on the situation.

"That's crazy. I can never believe how easy it is for people to get into bad situations when they are just minding their own business. Poor kid. Doesn't she have any family?"

"I guess she probably does in Jamaica, but she can't go back there right now, and there's nothing they could do to help with this. I don't think she's been back there since her aunt died."

"Poor kid." Lester repeated and then went back to explaining doorbell cameras and deadbolt locks.

Initially, Kestrel's blog, *SFUndertheRug.com*, had been about poking some fun at the wealthy and elite upper echelon of San Francisco. She delighted in uncovering their pettiness and pricking their little balloons of privilege. But, as the blog became more popular she had become aware of wanting to be sure she wasn't smearing the innocent with gossip, and that at least some part of her posts had been vetted by investigation. That is where Lester came in. It didn't hurt that Sam, the attorney, had suggested that she might want to cover her ass when she was poking fun at people without much sense of humor.

The blog and social media outlets had been fun, but at some point they had become lucrative. When she first began, the restaurants, hotels, sex shops, and other businesses had not been sure they wanted to be identified as the scenes of so much bullshit. However, when they started getting new business from people coming to check out the scene of the crime, so to speak, they started sending some advertising dollars Kestrel's way. It was nice to have the extra money, although she now required the occasional services of a part-time PI-cum-dramatic actor. She'd been doing some investing but had not changed her lifestyle much. Most of her ability to collect information on the wealthy was her invisibility to them. She continued to live her life as a server at the Pacific Union Club on Nob Hill, and The Towers. Her alter ego, K. Jones, quietly worked, waiting on and clearing up after people who didn't even notice she was there unless there was a problem. It was amazing how they behaved and talked in front of people they considered beneath their notice. It had been tricky to keep her name and photo out of the papers during criminal investigations she'd accidentally triggered, and especially the previous year when she'd become the unexpected beneficiary of an inheritance that had been highly contested in the courts. For that she had settled with the family, her family, for a lesser slice of the pie to keep from blowing her cover. She wasn't that interested in the money but was very interested in people not knowing her business. She liked what she did, although she felt a little sleazy sometimes. About the time she'd feel guilty some arrogant ass-hat would pull a dirty trick on someone she knew or show themselves to be a liar and a cheat and she would feel all noble and Robin Hood-ish again.

She still lived with reduced rent in one side of the duplex her mother owned and drove the old VW bug her mom had left behind when she moved on to other houses and cars. She could have paid her mother the full market rent, or moved to someplace better, but her relationship with Victoria was complicated, and it was better to keep it the way it was. She shuddered to think how Victoria would react to knowing she was the source of the popular blog, and her mom would have keeled over in a dead faint if she'd seen Kestrel's net worth.

Kestrel and Lester had finished their meeting before Beatrice emerged from the bathroom.

"Tell Beatrice the offer on the apartment is still on the table. I need to get it rented right away and places are hard to find in the city."

"I'll tell her. Let me know when you get that follow-up info."

Lester walked slowly to the bus stop, wondering what he could do to help Beatrice. As he got closer to his destination his pace quickened. He might not have a lot to offer a woman like that, but he did have some skills. It would be easy to find out a little more about Greta Gardner and her friends. Maybe there was something to help Beatrice's case. Something his research and PI skills would find that the police, who were focused on a quick arrest, might miss.

CHAPTER TWENTY-EIGHT

Okay, so maybe the building wasn't very impressive, and it was in a kind of crappy neighborhood, and it was on the third floor with no elevator, but it was roomy, with a lot of windows, even if most of the rooms were full of stuff and things were kind of messy. The thought of bringing Beatrice here to see it, and then breaking the news about how much half the rent was, made Lester cringe. San Francisco was no place to be looking for rental bargains. There were two bedrooms and one shared bath, which would definitely need some work. The kitchen wasn't bad, he thought. But it wasn't really good either. It had the necessary equipment if you mostly ate take-out and heated things up in the microwave. Shit. He was going to have to channel his dear old mother, big time, if this place was going to be made habitable. He briefly wondered why none of his previous roommates complained, but then he remembered that they were all ex-roommates. Maybe that was part of the problem. Well, if it got him an empty space for someone like Beatrice, he wasn't going to feel bad about it.

Before he set to work on the apartment, he spent some time doing research on Greta Gardner and her cadre of well-off friends, and while he was at it, he took a little look at Beatrice Campbell, originally from Jamaica through New York City.

Lester had an important audition the next day, a callback, so he gave up his cleaning project about three a.m. He thought he'd made some progress, but even he was surprised at the layers of grime and unexpected discoveries a little concentrated effort could uncover.

The next morning, he got up early, made a pot of coffee, and ran his lines for a few minutes. Some of his previous roomies had been actors, as well, and they'd been willing to help him with this, but this morning, he ran through them alone, imagining the actress that would be playing opposite him. The play was new, and he thought it wasn't half bad. The role was one he could knock out of the park, now he just needed to convince the director of that. He hadn't shaved in a couple of days and his stubble was pretty impressive. You didn't necessarily need to show up in any kind of costume, but he'd gotten more than one role by showing he understood the character in the way that he dressed for the audition.

When he left for the theater it was drizzling, and he thought about popping for an Uber instead of the bus. Money wasn't that tight, but then he thought that maybe a miserable trip across town with a couple of soggy bus-stop waits would help get him into character. By the time he got there he was cranky and wet. He sat in the warm green room with the other hopefuls and steam rose from his ratty trench coat. He had a cigarette in his pocket that was a little worse for wear that he thought might help give the impression he wanted today.

One by one the people around him were called onto the stage until it was only him and a woman wearing laddered tights, a very short black dress with Doc Marten boots, and a studded belt. She was buxom and both the top and bottom of her strained the fabric of the dress. Her tattoos were impressive. Finally, the stage manager called both Lester and the woman up to read through their scene. He heaved a sigh of relief when she uncrossed her legs and stood up from the battered couch she'd been occupying. She was only a little taller than he was. Sometimes you had to not just act your ass off but fight the urge to stand on your tiptoes to get past the height discrepancy. He felt even better about his chances when he got on the stage and realized she would be sitting at a table for the scene.

At just the right moment he drew the bent cigarette and a lighter from his pocket and pretended to light up. Of course, even for theater you couldn't smoke indoors, but he carried off the move with aplomb and finished his lines with just the right mix of despair and disillusionment. Hell, didn't anyone write comedies anymore? He'd had years of voice and dance lessons and ached for a chance at a musical, but everyone seemed so damned depressed, these days. Well, it didn't matter as long as you got the gig.

The director and his advisors did not dismiss Lester and the girl right away. They sat in the pool of light on the dark stage chatting amiably while the gods decided their fate. The girl was younger than she looked. Turned out her name was Amelia and she was a waitress at a place not too far from his apartment. He might have even seen her before. She told him that he probably wouldn't recognize her because they made her take out her nose, lip, and eyebrow studs and rings and cover her tats when she worked. Lester was very curious to see what she would look like without all the metalworks so he asked her when she was working again.

"I'm off the next couple of days but have a shift on Friday night." She smiled at him.

Damn, it was too bad she was so much younger than he was. He hadn't had a date in quite a while. "Maybe I'll stop by then. What time does your shift end?"

"I get off at ten. Maybe we could have a drink."

The director finally came up on the stage, gave them a couple of notes, and asked them to come back on Monday. Lester left feeling a lot cheerier than when he had arrived.

CHAPTER TWENTY-NINE

Bobby had just finished lunch with Raquel Stafford, the fraud cop he'd been dating for the past few months. Officially, just for the few months since her transfer from Homicide had been completed. It wasn't really considered kosher to be dating your co-workers in the same department. Not that there was much normal going on in their relationship. Raquel, or Rocky, as she was usually called, was a hardscrabble kind of gal who'd grown up in the projects of Oakland. She'd made a way for herself and wasn't one to back down, especially when it came to her career. Bobby, on the other hand, had a pretty normal Bay Area upbringing, still-married parents, college paid for, a cop from Internal Affairs who'd decided he'd rather deal with dead bodies than the crap he had seen in the department. As far as he could see his only failing was that he had a hankering for difficult women. Of course, Kestrel Jonas, his old girlfriend, and Rocky herself, could have probably reeled off a range of shortcomings, if he had bothered to ask.

For now, he knew his mother hoped he would settle down with one of the many young women she introduced him to and start cranking out grandbabies before she was too old to appreciate them. She thought he was almost perfect, except for that not-getting-married thing. She suspected he was dating someone, but he hadn't mentioned it or offered to bring anyone home for Sunday dinners or family holiday gatherings, no matter how much she hinted. So, she kept inviting single women from the church, relatives of her friends, and the occasional young teacher from the school she'd been secretary at for the past thirty years, since Bobby went there as a boy, to fill that empty chair at the family table.

Bobby had his own problems with invites these days. He thought he and Rocky were getting pretty serious. Serious enough that he'd been looking around at house listings in the Bay Area. Not in San Francisco, of course. Last he'd heard, there was a scandal about some guy who'd been paying $500 a month to live in a packing box in someone's apartment. He'd grown up in the North Bay, pretty rarefied territory, too, but was beginning to look in Rocky's East Bay stomping grounds. He didn't really care where he lived. He'd been camped out for the past few years in a bachelor pad that's most redeeming trait was its proximity to a corner bodega and a BART Station. Buying beer and getting to work easily were his priorities. Now there might be other things to think about. However, finding a place to live was not the problem. Getting Rocky to introduce him, or at least mention him, to her family was the problem. At first, when she was hesitant, he'd figured she didn't want him to meet her homies because she was embarrassed by them, but now he was beginning to suspect that she was embarrassed to introduce him to her family. Being white and fairly privileged, that possibility had not occurred to him until he'd tried discussing it with Kestrel.

"If we're both off this weekend we could go to Oakland and check out a couple of houses I found online. Maybe we could swing by your mom's while we're there," he said to Rocky.

"Um, I'm not sure I am going to be off this weekend."

"You said you definitely were off."

"Yes, well I guess I am. But my mom is not going to be around this weekend."

"The whole weekend? Is she going to be out of town?"

"I don't think so, but she's busy that day."

"We didn't set a day. We can do Saturday or Sunday. She must be home at least part of one of the days."

"Well, maybe. I'll have to check and get back to you."

Actually, they'd had almost this identical conversation several times lately, and it never worked out for him to meet her family. He could see that it might be awkward to just show up with this white boy at a family gathering, but how hard could it be to take her mom to lunch or stop by for a cup of coffee. He'd even bring donuts.

"Does your mother even know about me, Rocky?"

"Sure, she does. She knows I'm seeing someone."

"But does she know you are seeing me?"

"I'm pretty sure I've mentioned your name."

He could feel himself getting annoyed and decided to drop the subject, for now.

As they were leaving their favorite little greasy spoon: cheap, close to work, nothing fancy, Bobby's phone buzzed. He pulled the offending device from his pocket. "It's the coroner's office. Let me take this real quick." Rocky had no problem with that. Both of them were pretty much on call 24/7 in one way or another. She took the opportunity to take her own phone out and check for messages.

Bobby dialed the coroner back. "Yeah, this is Inspector Burns. I got a text that you had an update on the Gardner case."

Rocky could hear a garbled voice on the other end of Bobby's phone. It was that cute little coroner, Dr. Emma whatever-her-name-was. Word had it in the department that she was hot for Bobby Burns, but he'd never mentioned tapping that. Dr. Emma probably didn't know what Rocky had learned early in their relationship. He thought coroners were creepy. Score 1 for Rocky, 0 for Dr. Emma.

Bobby clicked off his phone and turned to Rocky. "I've got to go to the coroner's office and follow up on this. All my alibi checking was for nothing. The mode of delivery, the poison, was set up in advance. I've got to go find out where that puts us."

"Well, I'm headed back to the office. The trail on the scammer at UCSF is getting interesting now. At least we'll have something to talk about tomorrow."

"I thought we were having dinner tonight. I was going to cook."

"Um, sorry, it's my nephew Torey's birthday, so I have to go to Oakland."

"I'm good with birthday parties. I'll even bring a gift. A good gift... the best gift."

"Not tonight, Bobby. I'll make it up to you later." He hung onto her hand a little longer than necessary and she let him. She could sense his frustration but didn't really know what to say. She gave his hand a squeeze before she let go. With that Rocky turned and headed back to the office. Bobby watched her walk away. Talk about a fine ass…

Walking back to the station she gave some serious thought to what really was going on with her. Part of it was that she had never seriously dated a white dude before and it would cause some raised eyebrows in her family. Maybe she should point out that he wasn't exactly clamoring to take her home to meet his family, either. She loved her family, but they didn't dictate how she lived her life. If they had she would never have become a cop. If they could get past that one they could get past anything. As for Bobby, she'd seen him work and deal with people of every racial, ethnic, and social group and she'd never seen him treat anyone who deserved respect with disrespect. In fact, sometimes she thought he gave people too much benefit of the doubt. She didn't think he'd find her family weird or anything but who they were, and he would treat each of them that way. She wasn't as sure how they would treat him, but she knew that he could take it. What was getting in her way was that introducing him to her family would bring on all kinds of expectations. She hadn't brought a boyfriend home since she'd been fourteen years old. Of course, she'd had relationships, some of them pretty heavy, but once you took someone to meet the family the whole dynamic changed. She suspected, and had heard a few comments around the table, that some of her family just thought she was a lesbian and expected her to spring a girlfriend on them any time. They'd probably be relieved it was a guy she brought home. She just wasn't sure she was ready to be put in that position yet. But she didn't know how to explain that to Bobby.

It took just a few minutes for Bobby to reach the coroner's office. He didn't go in the main entrance where all the bereaved families congregated but went around to the loading dock. The officer at the desk recognized him and waved him through and he went in search of Dr. Kirschman, eventually finding her, sans protective gear, in the coffee area, pouring a cup of sludge and doctoring it appropriately with dried creamer and sugar. "You know, I used to think that sugar could cover up almost anything. You know, like 'a spoonful of sugar helps the medicine go down.'" She sang slightly off-key. "But there are some things it would take an entire sugar cane field and a trip to Hawaii to wipe the taste out of your mouth."

"I can imagine. What do you have for me on the Gardner case?"

"It was pretty clear from the beginning that it was cyanide poisoning; cherry-red skin, bitter almond smell, but it was a question of how it was administered, and when. There was a bottle of champagne and a glass, so that's where we looked first, but it became clear it was cyanide gas, and not ingested cyanide. The gas itself didn't kill her, but it caused her to pass out and the bath full of bubbles and scent did the rest. Her lungs were full of bath water, so she died of drowning, with help."

"You said that your findings blow the timing and alibis out of the water. What's that about?"

"When we began examining the articles in the bathroom, and interviewed her companion, we discovered that she habitually used candles and incense when she took a long leisurely soak. There was a jar of various incense cones and an Aladdin's lamp, a kind of brass burner for it. On examining it we discovered that the incense cone in the burner contained crystallized cyanide and the bath bomb she used likely contained cyanide and citric acid, which would have released the gas."

"What does that mean, exactly?"

"It means that at some time, any time, prior to the bath taken that night, someone placed contaminated incense cones and bath bombs in her home."

"So, the cyanide could have been introduced any time before that night?"

"Yes, the poison could have been placed there any time. Do we know when she obtained the bath items? Or, where they came from?"

"Nope, that's not one of the questions I thought to ask. I know who I can ask, though. So, you're saying that someone who knew she used incense and bath bombs, came into the bathroom and planted the cyanide there for the future. It didn't necessarily have anything to do with Saturday night?"

"Yep, that's what I'm saying. Do you want some coffee? It's pretty awful, but it will keep you awake the rest of the afternoon."

"No, thanks. I just had lunch and I have an unending supply of crappy coffee at my own office. This puts me back at square one. I have some possible suspects but I've wasted a couple of days now checking on alibis for Saturday night. Which all of them have."

"Sounds about right. Too bad, too. I got the victim's scans and labs from her cancer doctor and she was doing really well. She could have hung in for quite a while if someone hadn't decided to cut her life short for her."

"How could someone poison someone with incense and bath water?"

"It wouldn't be that difficult. In fact, it's kind of ingenious. Cyanide gas is released if the solid is either burned or dissolved. Water will work, but acid will be even more potent. So, bath bombs don't have water in them, but they have citric acid, so when they are dropped into the water they start to release the gas. Along with the compressed, also waterless, incense cone, it released enough to knock our victim out. It might have killed her if she hadn't slipped down into the water and drowned."

"But cyanide isn't that easy to get, is it? And, wouldn't it be dangerous to work with?"

"You can find instructions for making it on the Internet and you can buy small amounts of it there, as well. I wouldn't want to be messing with it, but a trained chemist could probably handle it fairly safely, especially in small amounts."

Bobby didn't answer right away. He was already moving on to the next round of interviews and the first thing that had been triggered in his mind was who stood to benefit from Greta Gardner's death? She didn't have any family; no kids or living husbands. Where exactly was her money going to go now, and who didn't want to wait? "Thanks for the updates, Doc."

"Please, call me Emma." She really did have a cute smile.

"Emma, thanks for everything. I'm off to see if I can find out who was going to directly benefit, sooner rather than later, from Ms. Gardner's death.

CHAPTER THIRTY

Bobby stopped by the station to get his car and ducked into his office to check on things. Sergeant Morris hunched in her chair glumly staring at the monitor.

"Morris, have we gotten anything back on the robot vacuums on Walnut Street?"

She picked up a file folder from her desk and handed it to him without looking away from the computer. "Report's in here. Usual house dirt."

"What are you looking at?"

"Just checking the doorbell cameras and security tapes from Ms. Gardner's neighbors over that weekend. Pretty boring."

"Yeah, well, get used to it. Looks like we need to go much further back. Get the recordings going back at least a month if you can. We're looking for anybody delivering or bringing something to the house."

Finally, she looked directly at him, and it was not a cheerful sight.

After a moment she just shrugged and stood up. "I'll need to go back to the neighbors, then."

"While you're there, go into the house and get a crew out there to open the wall safe, it's in the bedroom in the back of one of the cabinets." He dropped the folder on his own desk. "Do you have the address of the Gardner woman's attorney? I need to talk to him."

Morris rummaged through a few papers and copied the name and address on a neon pink sticky note for him.

Bobby took the note from her. "Call the attorney's office and tell them I'm on my way and need information on Gardner's estate…please." He stopped for a moment to consider the young woman before him. She wasn't very impressive to look at, but she always got things done, efficiently, if not cheerfully. He couldn't recall if he'd ever seen her smile in the weeks since she'd been assigned to work with him. "You're doing a great job, Morris. Thanks for your help." Was that the slightest glimmer of a smile? Not really, but the scowl around her eyebrows did lift a bit.

"Thank you, sir."

Bobby didn't have any trouble finding the attorney's address on Van Ness, but parking was another issue. He circled the maze of one-way streets for several minutes before he found a parking garage that claimed to still have a few open spots. In movies and on TV there's always a parking spot out front when a cop needs one, but in real life, not so much.

The offices of Addison and Mitchell were not impressive except for their deep grounding in tradition and solidity: Heavy wood paneling, plush carpets, dark portraits of previous partners. Gordon Addison's receptionist was another thing. She was definitely not the prim Miss Grundy he'd expected, but a svelte and leggy woman he'd have liked to know better.

"Mr. Addison is expecting you, Inspector Burns. I'll just ring you in." She spoke quietly into the phone receiver and then a buzz and click sounded from the heavy door to her right.

Mr. Addison was not really what Bobby expected, either. He was on the youngish side of middle age, blond, tanned, and imposing. "Inspector Burns, I've had Ms. Gardner's file brought in so we can discuss her estate." He hesitated for a moment. "It's rather shocking that she's been murdered; she was just in here the other day and seemed almost her old self."

"Yes, I understand she'd been responding to treatment and was feeling better."

"Please sit down." Mr. Addison seated himself behind the massive desk and opened the file before him. "There isn't really anything surprising in her estate paperwork. She'd been very thorough in setting everything up in light of her recent illness."

"I understand that she came into the office to make some changes."

"Yes, she was here to finalize some changes she'd requested, but nothing really significant."

"What kind of changes?"

"You have to understand her estate is quite large. She inherited money from her parents and from both of her husbands, had no children or siblings, and was a fairly savvy investor, so even if the dollar amounts of her bequests seem large, they were just a small part of the big picture."

"Was Ms. Gardner someone who made frequent changes?"

"Not at all. It had been several years since she'd made substantive changes. Her fortune had increased quite a lot since the last papers were signed and, of course, her real estate holdings had skyrocketed."

Bobby could see that Gordon Addison was not the least bit concerned with this interview, and Gordon Addison could see that Bobby Burns didn't want to be hanging out here all day.

"Inspector, why don't I go over the basic will and trust prior to changes and then highlight what was changed? That is probably the most straightforward."

Bobby sat back prepared to listen and hoping to hear something that would help him move forward on this case.

Greta Gardner did indeed have a large fortune, even by California standards, and she'd not been a big spender. Oh, she'd lived a nice life, but nothing really flashy. When she did invest it was in solid companies and especially in San Francisco real estate. While there were a few bequests of personal property to old friends, her instructions were to sell everything she owned and distribute the money as directed, with Mr. Addison as the executor of her estate. Her old friend, Bertram Frankel, would receive the proceeds of a large trust fund until his death at which time the trust fund would be distributed to a charitable organization of her choosing. The documents said the money was so that Mr. Frankel "would be able to maintain his lifestyle for the rest of his days." Most of the rest of her fortune was apportioned out as percentages to a number of charities and artistic foundations.

"The recent changes just redistributed some of the proceeds and added a couple of beneficiaries. One of them was a medical non-profit and the other a personal friend."

Gordon Addison straightened the papers neatly and slid them back into the file folder. "Do you have any questions, Inspector?"

"Just a couple. Are you also Mr. Frankel's attorney?"

"Mr. Frankel is a client of this firm, although one of the other associates handles his business."

"Well, at least that makes it pretty easy to keep on top of all of this."

Addison nodded assent to that.

Bobby stood to leave. "One more thing, do you know who handles Mr. Frankel's financial affairs? He must have an accountant or someone."

"Yes, Carlton Drummond is his financial adviser. I think Ms. Grant has one of his cards; we often refer clients to his firm. He and I went to school together."

The attorney stood and escorted Bobby to the door and into the outer office. "Ms. Grant, please give Inspector Burns one of Carlton Drummond's cards." Turning back to Bobby he shook his hand, again. "Please let me know if you need any additional information. I hope you are able to find this killer. Ms. Gardner deserved to have peace in whatever time was left to her."

Bobby thought the man sounded sincere, and he nodded in agreement.

CHAPTER THIRTY-ONE

On Friday Beatrice woke from a sound sleep full of dreams. The dream had started in Jamaica, a place she longed for but feared to visit. It moved to New York City, then on to San Francisco, with her watching the man from the mortuary moving her Auntie Bea out of the apartment, not on a gurney, but by lifting her in his arms and carrying her out to a station wagon like a groom carrying his bride across the threshold. The alarm on her phone rang for several seconds before she was able to pull herself up from her dream to discover what that annoying noise was. She realized it was her phone and picked it up noting it was the alarm for the Cancer Center appointment Greta was supposed to have today. "Shit, I didn't notify them that she wouldn't be coming," she thought. She doubted it would matter and was about to turn over and go back to sleep when Kestrel stumbled out of the bedroom, awakened by the squawking alarm.

"What was that noise?" She yawned.

"I'm sorry, it was the alarm I set so I could get Ms. Gardner to her doctor's appointment today. I forgot to cancel it."

"Are you going to go?"

"No, why would I go?"

"I don't know. I was just thinking that it might be worth going over there and seeing if anybody there knows anything."

Beatrice just looked at Kestrel and shook her head. "Nobody there ever came to the house or would have any reason to hurt Greta."

"You don't really know that. Didn't you say she'd heard from someone about her test results?"

"Yeah, but he must have called her. The study coordinator, Sandeep. She called him Sandy. I think she was kind of sweet on him."

"What time is the appointment?"

"It's at ten this morning. It took a lot of time to get Greta put together and over there."

"Well, it won't take that much time for us to get ready, but we'll be taking the bus instead of driving."

Beatrice sighed. She was getting very tired of this whole thing. She'd hoped she'd never have to see that cancer center again, but she supposed it was possible that someone there would know something. But she couldn't imagine what it would be. Still, the people there had been very kind to Greta and she didn't even know if anyone had told them that she was dead. They shouldn't find out from the police. They dealt with life and death every day and seemed to really care that the patients would benefit from their treatment.

Getting up she thought that she especially should try to speak directly with Sandeep, as he'd dealt with Greta most closely.

Kestrel had gone back into the bedroom to dress but stuck her head out the door. "Tell you what, we'll go to the cancer center and then we'll catch lunch at a little place I know near there."

Just as they were getting ready to leave Beatrice got a call from Lester. "Sorry, Lester. Kestrel and I are going to the cancer center to talk to the staff there and then going to lunch. Really? I didn't realize your apartment is close to the cancer center. Wait a minute, I'll check."

She turned to Kestrel, "Lester wants me to look at the apartment today. Can he meet us for lunch and then we can go to his place?"

Kestrel shrugged, "Sure, let me talk to him a minute. Lester, we'll be going to Rasta Reggae on Third Street, in Mission Bay. I'll let you know when we leave the cancer center and you can meet us there, and you can buy us lunch." She handed the phone back to Beatrice. "Let's get going."

The bus let them off right in front of the medical building Beatrice had been to so many times. She hesitated as she looked at the broad doors. She took a deep breath, "Okay, let's get this over with."

The waiting room had not changed since the last time she was there. A number of the people she'd seen before were there, some of them participants in the clinical trial Greta had been in. Some of them were missing. It made her feel better to think that it was because they had gotten better and didn't need to show up here anymore. She wondered if any of those there today were wondering where Greta was. They'd formed a bond of hope and desperation, but not the kind where you got together away from here. Their conversations had centered on the study and their illness. They would be wondering why she wasn't here, but nobody would ask.

She and Kestrel walked up to the check-in window. The usual distracted nurse didn't even look up from the computer. "Can I have your name, please?"

"Beatrice Campbell, but…"

The nurse raised her hand to silence Beatrice and typed the name into the computer. "I'm not seeing you in our system." Still not looking up. "What time is your appointment?"

Getting annoyed, Kestrel stepped ahead of Beatrice. "Excuse me…" she looked at the nametag on the woman's ample bosom "…Michelle. But, we are here about Ms. Greta Gardner's appointment."

The startled woman looked up. "You can't come to an appointment in place of a patient."

"Yes, we know that, but Ms. Gardner—" she glanced around and lowered her voice to a whisper "—passed away over the weekend. We need to talk to the person who is running the study."

"That would be Sandeep Sheik. He's with a study subject right now. This will have to be reported as an SAE."

"An SAE?"

"Serious Adverse Event, on the study."

Kestrel leaned in closer to Michelle. "The police are investigating it as a murder."

"Oh dear, I don't know how to report that kind of SAE. I'll have to call the study sponsor."

"Okay, but we need to talk to Sandeep."

"You're not the police, are you?"

Beatrice decided it was time to take back control. Kestrel was just confusing things. "Michelle, you remember me. I came here all the time with Ms. Gardner. I was her companion and assistant when she came in."

Michelle looked more closely at Beatrice. "Yes, I remember you coming in with her. But, I still don't know why you need to talk to Sandeep."

"Michelle, I'm sure you know how sad I am at what has happened. I just want to talk to him about whether Greta, Ms. Gardner, mentioned any concerns or worries with him."

"He can't talk to you about the study or her medical condition. That is protected by HIPAA laws."

"I know, I just think they were friendly and she might have mentioned something to him if she was afraid or anything."

Michelle kind of rolled her eyes at that. "Yes, well, Sandeep is very friendly with a lot of the subjects, the female ones, at least." She realized she should not have added that last part so she clammed up, turned in her chair, and stood. "I'll let Mr. Sheik know that you are here and see if he has a few minutes to talk to you. We're very busy." Michelle hustled away, disappearing down a long hallway.

Kestrel and Beatrice sat down in a couple of standard-issue waiting room chairs. This was Kestrel's first experience of the look and feel of long-term medical care. The people ranged around the room were either rather-the-worse-for-wear patients or their hovering attendants. Some were parents taking care of children, some were children taking care of parents. Spouses supporting one another and occasionally, single people, huddled in chairs, arms wrapped around themselves, trying to keep it together for whatever the day would bring. The cheerful colors and bright artwork of the downstairs lobby and hallways had faded away in this room. The stylish chairs were replaced by whatever had been left over from the last remodel. Donors didn't come here; this place was not made to impress. Kestrel thought it was more designed to depress.

CHAPTER THIRTY-TWO

After a couple of minutes Michelle returned to her sentry post and continued to check in patients. Probably fifteen minutes later a middle-aged, good-looking man, dressed in dark scrubs hurried into the waiting room and looked around anxiously. His eyes lit on Kestrel and Beatrice on the first sweep of the room, as they stood out from the usual inhabitants. He walked briskly to them. "Good morning, I am Sandeep Sheik, Ms. Gardner's study coordinator. I understand you want to speak with me."

Kestrel and Beatrice both stood up, but Kestrel responded first. "Yes. This is Ms. Campbell, Ms. Gardner's companion, and I am her friend, Ms. Jonas."

Sandeep shook their hands in turn but continued to just stand there waiting for them to tell him what they wanted. Finally, Beatrice said, "Mr. Sheik, I don't think it is appropriate to discuss this matter in a public waiting room. Do you have a space we can use?"

It was obvious that Sandeep did not want to escort them to his private space, but he couldn't immediately think of any reason not to. "Of course, please follow me." He spun on his heel and strode quickly down the long hallway with Kestrel and Beatrice trailing behind him.

Neither of them had previously experienced the labyrinth that comprises most back offices in medical facilities. At the end of the hall, he abruptly turned right, then left, then past two elevators, and finally down a tiny passage to a closed door that he unceremoniously opened. If the waiting room was grim, this space was downright pathetic. The room had been recently painted but the color reminded Kestrel of the free paint her mother had once acquired at a paint recycling center. The color was a non-color. Whatever hue it is that paint is before it actually acquires a real color, with whatever leftover pigment it was impossible to remove tingeing it with a smoky undertone.

The small space contained a desk of the gray metal variety and two metal chairs with the seats and backs' upholstery haphazardly repaired with duct tape. There was a bookshelf that contained fat white binders crammed with forms and papers, and a huge stack of patient files teetered on the edge of the desk. The computer was of the outdated clunky variety where the CPU took up half the space under the desk. She could see that the tall man must have to scrunch himself all out of whack to sit and work at the computer with his legs under the desk, scrabbling away in the harsh light from the fluorescent tubes above him.

He sat in the only free chair in the room, the other chair being piled with binders and files. "How can I help you? I don't have a lot of time."

Just as Beatrice was about to speak someone tapped on the door.

"Yes?" the man responded.

The door opened and a woman's head poked in. "Sandy, I will need some time with you this afternoon to go over the corrections in the EDC Database for the COSMOS study."

"Yes, that's fine. We can meet after lunch. Will it take long?"

"Well, not too long. A lot of your data hasn't been entered yet, so I'll probably have to arrange to come back next week if you'll be able to get everything updated."

Sandeep huffed out a sigh. "We are the highest enroller in your study, so it is very difficult to see all the study subjects and keep caught up with the data."

The woman just looked at him. Kestrel could see that she'd love to tell him that study data was what he got paid for, but, she was only a lowly worker bee, so she didn't say it. Her boss would have to tell his boss that the data entry needed to be stepped up. In the meantime, she needed his cooperation if she was going to get her job done. She smiled sympathetically. "I know, but we really want to lock the database before long and do some analysis. Things are looking pretty good."

When the door had closed behind the woman, Sandeep turned to them again. "Now, please tell me what this is about."

"I came here to tell you that Ms. Gardner will not be here for her appointment today."

"Why on earth not?" Sandeep could not keep the annoyance out of his voice.

"Well, because she's dead. She died on Saturday night, and I forgot to let you know until my alarm went off today."

"Dead? What happened? We will need to report this to the study sponsor and the FDA."

"It was not anything related to her disease or her treatment. The police think she was murdered."

"The police?"

Kestrel could detect the hint of alarm in his voice.

"The police may come here to talk to you, but in case they don't, I wanted you to know that she wouldn't be coming back."

Sandeep sat back in his chair and threw up his hands. "I don't know what to make of this. I'm going to need documentation and details for my SAE report. Who do I talk to about that?"

"I'm not sure. I guess the police or the coroner, I don't know."

"Do you know what happened?"

"I found her in the bathtub," Beatrice said. "It looked like she might have just died there, but the coroner said it looked suspicious. That's all I really know."

Sandeep seemed like he might ask more questions, but after a moment he stood up. "You can't really give me the information I need for the sponsor. I will have to see what I can find out some other way. Do you have the name of the police person I should talk to?"

"Yes, I have his name and number." Kestrel gave him the information for reaching Bobby, only slightly concerned that Bobby was going to be pissed off that she had been here. There was nothing she could do about that now.

Sandeep did not escort them back to the waiting room, just ushered them into the narrow passage and closed his office door behind them. It took them a couple of wrong turns to find their way back to the waiting room and make their way out of the building.

CHAPTER THIRTY-THREE

The little Jamaican restaurant that Kestrel had found was just a few blocks from the cancer center so they walked there quickly. She'd called Lester to tell him they were headed that way and they enjoyed their stroll down the street. The place was definitely a hole-in-the-wall but had recently been featured on a hugely popular food show that showcased good food in unusual places. Kestrel hoped not only that the food was good, but that it would cheer Beatrice up.

Reggae Rasta was one step up from what she'd have called a dive, but seemed to be one of those places that were a passion project for someone who knew what they were doing with the traditional foods of their homeland. The décor was bright and the music had a cheerful beat to it. Signs in the window indicated that the special of the day was jerk chicken with collard greens and that live music was available on Wednesday and Saturday evenings. All in all, Kestrel felt good about her choice.

As they entered the small café Beatrice was already bopping to the beat of the familiar music and enjoying the bright paintings on the wall. "Oh, I love this place. I didn't even know it was here."

"Just took a little work on the Internet. I don't know anything about Jamaican food. What is the best thing you can think of?"

"Goat, oh my God, I hope they have goat. Oh, and plantains."

Goat and plantains were not exactly what Kestrel was hoping to get for lunch. But she might be willing to give it a try after such an enthusiastic recommendation.

The woman behind the counter waved her arm around the room. "Sit anywhere ya' want." She smiled. They took seats at the front window so they could watch for Lester, their meal ticket, and plucked the menus from the napkin/salt/pepper/hot sauce stand on the table.

"Oh, they do have goat!"

"Yeah, great!"

The waitress, the same woman from behind the counter, had taken their drink orders and they were poring over the menu, Beatrice with somewhat more enthusiasm than Kestrel, when Lester came through the front door.

"Good day, ladies. You made good time getting here. This place looks great. I live just a couple blocks away and I've never noticed it before. That's one great thing about this neighborhood, I'm always discovering something new."

Kestrel looked askance at this new Lester. He sounded, and looked, like a used car salesman trying to unload that 1999 Oldsmobile on the back lot.

Kestrel moved to the chair near the window to make room for Lester but instead he went around Beatrice so he could sit next to her, only having to move two other chairs and squeeze through the narrow opening.

"Beatrice was just celebrating that this place serves goat."

"Wow…goat…I may have to try that." Lester smiled broadly.

"They have so many of the things I remember from when I was a kid."

"Well, then. You'll have to tell us what all of this is and make some recommendations." Lester had picked up the menu and was looking at it quizzically.

The waitress came back to get their orders, bringing drinks for Kestrel and Beatrice. "What will it be for you good folks today?"

"Beatrice, why don't you go first?"

"Great, I would like the curry goat if it is made with yams Otherwise, I want the jerk chicken special."

"Of course, we use yams in our goat curry Do you want the half portion or the full portion?"

"The full portion please, and a side of plantains."

Kestrel lifted her head from the menu having finally found an item that she recognized, and was willing to eat all the listed ingredients. "I'll have the jerk chicken, but without collards. Oh, and fries." As far as Kestrel was concerned anything was improved by the addition of French fries.

Lester tamped down his trepidation and piped up "I'll have what this lovely young lady is having." He inclined his head toward Beatrice.

"Good, that's two full portion orders of goat curry and two sides of plantains with an order of jerk chicken but without the collards, and one order of fries.. What would the gentleman like to drink?"

"Can I get a beer, a large beer, or maybe two beers." Lester figured you could eat almost anything if you could wash it down with beer.

Beatrice was feeling much better today and chattered away about her childhood in Jamaica, the artwork on the walls, and her favorite comfort foods. Lester hung on her words but Kestrel had clocked out at about the third Auntie Bea story and was thinking about the murder of Greta Gardner and wondering what she could do to help her friend. It seemed to her that, although Beatrice was upset, it was more about the death of her friend and employer. Kestrel knew from past experience that you could be completely innocent and still need to worry about how things were being seen.

CHAPTER THIRTY-FOUR

The server brought two beers and their food orders to the table just as Kestrel's phone rang. "Bobby, how are you? Yes, Beatrice is with me. Her phone must be off or on silent." She listened for a moment, not allowing any expression to dim the smile on her face. "We are just about to have lunch. Can I have her call you back in a few minutes when she can get some privacy? Cool, thanks. No, I won't forget, she just heard me and nodded, so both of us know she needs to call you."

Kestrel took a moment to compose herself as she looked down to slip her phone back into her purse.

"That was Inspector Burns? He was trying to reach me?" Beatrice had pulled her own phone from her pocket. "Oh my, it's dead, I think. I must have forgotten to charge it last night."

"No worries. You can call him back on my phone after lunch. Your stew smells wonderful. What does it have in it, besides goat, I mean?"

Beatrice had eagerly scooped up a spoonful of the dish before her. "It has yams and okra. My grandma used to grow okra in her backyard and me and my cousins would go pick it for her when she made this dish."

Lester was taking a more sedate approach to the meal set before him. He placed a napkin in his lap and took up his spoon. "It really does smell delicious." He also thought it looked very suspicious. Lots of brown with a few bits of orange, white, and green peeking out from the pottage. At least he could recognize the carrots and yams and guessed the green was the okra that Beatrice was talking about. He scooped a meager half spoonful of the mixture up and, taking a deep breath, put it into his mouth. His hand was already reaching for the first beer bottle in case he needed it in a hurry. "Wow, it tastes delicious, too." He pulled the beer-reaching hand back and picked a piece of the fresh bread from the basket on the table.

Lester did his best to keep the conversation going but the call from the police had put a damper on his companions' enthusiasm. Finally, he stopped trying and concentrated on his food and beer.

It was evidence of her naïveté that Beatrice had not asked what Bobby wanted. He'd told Kestrel he needed to talk to Beatrice about Ms. Gardner's will.

When they had finished eating and Lester was nursing the last of his second beer, Kestrel handed her phone to Beatrice. "Bea, why don't you make your call outside while Lester and I finish. That way you have some privacy."

Beatrice took the phone and stepped out the door onto the sunny sidewalk. This was not one of those teeming city streets where you'd have to huddle for quiet, though the traffic noise caused her to plug her free ear as she began talking on the phone.

"What is going on?" Lester leaned across the table toward Kestrel.

"I'm not sure. He has some questions about Ms. Gardner's will. I don't know if Beatrice knows anything about that or not."

"Look, I've been checking Beatrice's background and I have a couple of questions, myself."

"Why would you be checking her background, Lester? Are you trolling her or something?"

"I'm not trolling anybody. You and I both know that what I am doing is exactly what the police are doing except that they are doing it to find a reason to charge her. I'm doing it to prevent that. Shhh, here she comes."

Beatrice came back through the door of the cheerful café looking much less happy than when she left.

She sat down on the edge of the chair and distractedly handed the phone back to Kestrel. "Inspector Burns said he talked to Greta's attorney and that Greta changed her will recently and left me quite a bit of money."

Kestrel and Lester's first reactions were to be happy for Beatrice, but then reality set in and they realized that an inheritance could be construed as a motive for murder.

Beatrice didn't know what to think. She'd never discussed the will or money with Greta. She assumed Greta had quite a lot of money and knew that she periodically pulled all her files out of the safe in her bedroom and went through them making notes and talking to herself. Beatrice never asked about it and Greta never mentioned it or explained.

"What did Bobby say, exactly?"

"He said that he had talked to the attorney who told him the will had recently been changed and that Greta had put a bequest to me into it."

"Did he say whether any other changes were made to the will?"

"No, and I didn't think to ask him about it."

"How much money?" Lester couldn't resist.

"I don't know. I was so surprised I didn't ask. He said a lot of money, but I guess I don't know what that really means."

They were all silent for a few minutes, deep in their own thoughts. Finally, Lester took his last gulp of beer and stood up. "Why don't you two go outside in the sunshine while I settle the tab here?" He was grateful that Kestrel had chosen a mid-range cafe so he didn't have to lay out a big chunk of change for lunch.

"Are you ready to go check out the apartment? It's just a couple of blocks from here."

As they walked the short distance Lester was careful to point out the advantages of the neighborhood. The convenient BART Station and bus stops, the used bookstore, the corner bodega. He was equally as careful to leave the homeless sleeping in the doorways and the sinister gathering of gang members on one of the corners out of the conversation.

"Here we are." They stopped at a heavily gated, narrow doorway that opened to a long flight of dark, narrow stairs. "It's not as bad as it looks." Kestrel and Beatrice peered up into the dimness. "Usually there are lights on here. I forgot to turn them on when I left."

Lester led the way up the steps with Kestrel and Beatrice following him single file up the narrow passage. Kestrel was just glad that it did not smell and seemed pretty clean.

Lester already had the key in his hand when they reached the two doors at the top of the flight of stairs and turned to the door on the right. "Ta-dah!" He flung the door open and the three of them jostled through it into the tiny entry.

The apartment itself was bright and neat. In fact, Kestrel was thinking she ought to hire Lester to clean her place. His was much neater than hers and all the surfaces glowed from the recent attention they'd received. Of course, neither she nor Beatrice knew the hours Lester had spent making the place presentable. He didn't have "designs" on Beatrice as much as he just thought that another distant, male roommate who snuck smokes in the bathroom and missed the toilet 80% of the time when he peed would drive him over the brink. A lovely person, who laughed and read, and loved children and cooked goat, or whatever else she wanted to, on the weekend might save him.

CHAPTER THIRTY-FIVE

The outing had been great but Kestrel and Beatrice returned to the duplex exhausted. They were really too tired to think about dinner, and at least one of them was still stuffed with goat stew. Kestrel poured them a couple of glasses of wine and they curled up on the chair and couch and read. Actually, Kestrel was hoping that Beatrice would go to bed early. The deck could be reached both from the living room and the single bedroom. Kestrel had noted that Sam's lights were on and she hoped to slip out onto the deck from her room and climb over the low railing between her deck and Sam's. She wanted to talk to him about Greta's will and see if he thought Beatrice might need to hire a lawyer. She also wanted to talk to Lester more. She didn't know what he might have uncovered in checking out Beatrice, but she feared for her friend.

Beatrice was actually just pretending to read, curled up on the end of the sofa. She had a book open, but she was confused by having received three texts in the past hour offering her jobs with other wealthy people in

San Francisco. It appeared that there was a small subset of vetted household help/companions among the elite of the city. When the word got around that Greta had died people had been scrambling for Beatrice's phone number. She'd worked for the Spencer family and now for Greta Gardner; she was a known quantity among a group of rich, particular, and slightly paranoid socialites. Was socialite even a word anymore? She had sent vague responses to the texts. She needed a job, but she didn't want to mislead anyone about her circumstances.

At least not any more than she was already misleading people. She slid her glance in Kestrel's direction wondering when she might stop reading and go to bed so Beatrice could make some private phone calls.

In fact, Beatrice was not the only one in the room surreptitiously sending texts. Earlier in the day, after the bombshell about the will, Kestrel had sent a text to Bobby asking him if anything else had been recently changed in Greta's will. She'd also been in touch with Lester. She wasn't sure if you still called it a tongue-lashing when it took place through messaging, but she was really upset that he was stalking poor Beatrice. She could tell he liked the woman, but hell, they were supposed to be her friends, not checking up on her. Basically, Lester told her to chill out and get a grip, which just pissed her off more.

Beatrice closed the book whose page she had not turned once in the past hour, stretched broadly and yawned. "Well, I'm beat. I'm going to change into my jammies and brush my teeth."

"Finally," Kestrel thought. She closed her book and stood up. While Beatrice had the bathroom door closed she grabbed a new bottle of wine and two glasses and set them on the deck outside the bedroom. She had texted Sam to unlock his slider and had the satisfaction of hearing the lock click while she was setting the wine on the deck. It was kind of fun sneaking out again like she had in school. Although, truth be told, Victoria had been more likely to be hiding something in those days than Kestrel was. She'd given up counting the number of times she'd seen someone sneaking down the back steps of the deck at her mom's house at six a.m. The little path that ran from the back door, across the deck, down the steps and around the house to the driveway was well traveled. For a number of years Kestrel had carefully placed a bolster and some blankets in her bed forming a reasonable facsimile of her sleeping self, until she realized that her mother would not ever think to peek in to check on her and find her bed empty. After that she fell into the habit of writing insulting notes to her mother and leaving them on the empty bed, quite confident that they would never be read. Looking back on it was kind of sad, but Kestrel liked to believe that she had come to terms with all those demons, long ago.

Sam had hardly lifted his head from the files and books stacked on his dining table for hours when he'd received Kestrel's text. This latest pro bono case he'd been working on was taking all his time and more energy than he really had at the end of a long week. Most of the weekend would be spent reviewing, revising, organizing, and praying before he went to court next week to plead for a man's innocence.

He sighed and pushed the papers away from himself and went to unlock the slider. A bottle of wine and listening to Kestrel's adventures would be a welcome respite.

While he waited for her to arrive he straightened his table, put on some smooth jazz, went into the bathroom to straighten himself out a bit, as well. The sight in the mirror was not reassuring. The jeans and T-shirt were clean enough but looked sloppy. Kestrel had told him once that he looked more like a sad clown than a successful lawyer; success being a relative term in his case. His own dad thought he was the waste of a perfectly good law degree, but he just couldn't bring himself to care about the woes of a bunch of wealthy clients who all deserved a slap back into reality as far as he was concerned. He spent his energy, time, and sometimes his money, in the interest of other sad sacks like himself.

Kestrel, and his sisters, had told him that dressing a bit cooler and getting a decent haircut might help him get a girlfriend, but he wasn't sure he wanted a girl who cared about those things. He'd turned away from the mirror and switched off the bathroom light when he heard the door slide open. "Hey, Kestrel. Thanks for saving me from myself."

Kestrel waved the wine bottle in his direction. "You may not thank me when you hear what's going on."

"What kind of predicament did you get yourself into this time?"

"Not me, Beatrice. I'm not sure what to think. That's why I need to talk to you." Kestrel sat on the end of the couch and swung her bare feet up onto it while Sam opened the wine and filled the wineglasses she'd brought. She knew him well. The closest thing to wineglasses he had were some juice cups she'd given him for his birthday in a hopeless attempt to stop him from drinking from the jug in the fridge.

It only took the first glass of wine to get through the Beatrice-related facts: finding the body, being named in the will, whatever interesting information Lester had dug up on her. Sam poured them each a second glass before he sat back in his chair with a furrowed brow. "If this was an episode of *Father Brown,* Beatrice would already be charged and getting spiritual advice from the good father."

Kestrel nodded. One thing she and Sam shared was an addiction to British murder mysteries. "It's a good thing for her that Bobby is not the police chief in Kembleford."

"Ah, yes, Bobby Burns. I'm guessing he is not thrilled to have you involved in his case."

"I'm not involved. Well…not very involved, anyway."

Sam just looked at her and shook his head.

CHAPTER THIRTY-SIX

Lester hesitated outside Kestrel's door. He knew that she wasn't there as he'd specifically planned to visit when only Beatrice would be home. Now, though, he wasn't feeling quite so confident about what he would say.He took a deep breath, squared his shoulders, and knocked.

Beatrice answered almost immediately. It looked like she'd been cleaning house; her hair was wrapped up in a scarf and she was wearing an apron. She must have brought her own, as Lester doubted Kestrel owned such an item of clothing. The strong scent of pine cleaner wafter over him from the open doorway.

"Oh, Lester, hello. I'm sorry but Kestrel isn't here. She's working today. I just thought I would clean up a bit and surprise her." Beatrice raised her yellow rubber-gloved hands.

"That's good, I mean, it's okay that Kestrel's not here. I actually wanted to talk to you privately."

Beatrice looked surprised. "Privately?"

"I brought donuts." Lester held up a greasy paper bag.

Beatrice laughed, "Well, never let it be said that I turned away a guest bearing sugary gifts." She stepped back and motioned for him to enter as she pulled the rubber gloves from her hands.

Lester handed the bag to Beatrice and rested his laptop bag against the leg of the kitchen table.

Beatrice had pulled a plate from the cabinet and turned on the electric kettle, her own addition to the kitchen amenities. "Why do you need to talk to me privately, Lester?"

"It's about something I discovered in my research, about you and your Aunt."

Beatrice's back visibly stiffened and she stood very still, facing the counter. "Why would you be researching me and my aunt?"

"It isn't something creepy, I promise. I just knew that the police would be doing the same research at some point and wanted to make sure we knew what questions might come up."

After a moment, Beatrice began the motions of making tea and laying the doughnuts out on a plate. The delectable scent of grease and sugar rose from the plate. "And what did you find out?"

"I found out a few things, but the most amazing one is how young you look for your age."

Beatrice turned to look at him. "And what is my age, Lester?"

"Well according to the passport you used to enter the United States, twenty years ago, you are 45 years old and you look almost exactly the same now as you did then. And your niece's passport from ten years ago looks almost the same as you look now."

Beatrice set the plate of pastries on the table and sank into one of the chairs. "My niece did look a lot like me."

"I am not here to give you any trouble Beatrice, I just want to help make sure that no questions come up about your citizenship, or any secrets you might have." Lester wanted to reach out and take her hand across the table but sat down in the chair opposite her and waited to see what she would say.

Beatrice sat frozen in her chair until the whistle on the teakettle went off. She stood, turned to the counter, and made them each a cup of tea before she spoke again.

"When I was very young my Aunt Beatrice moved to NYC and I was left behind in Jamaica. My mother was gone and Daddy was ill and needed me to take care of him. He died when I was 20 and Aunt Beatrice asked me to come visit her. She was working as a nanny but had her own apartment and we were doing well, although I was supposed to go back to Jamaica before long. We had hoped that she could bring me here permanently with a family visa, but a niece isn't close enough relation and there is a long, long waiting list. Even though I had no family left in Kingston I was going to have to go back and be on my own."

Beatrice stirred her tea, absently, "Then, Aunt Beatrice found out she was very sick. At that same time the children she'd been taking care of were sent to boarding school and she needed to find another job. She decided that she would relocate to San Francisco where nobody knew her. She brought me with her, and when she went to a doctor she gave him my name. She began applying for nanny jobs here and I was the one who went for the interviews. When she died we told the coroner that it was me who had passed and I took the nanny job with the Spencer family. They hadn't needed me right away because they were just expecting twins and the job did not start until they were born, so I was able to take care of her for the last few months.

While Beatrice was speaking Lester had opened his computer and accessed some of the information he'd found. He turned the laptop to face Beatrice. "Here's what I found. I am no techno wizard so it is pretty basic stuff, but I think it needs to be "polished" a bit to make sure no questions are raised by the police."

"What do you mean, polished?"

"Let me ask you something before I answer that. Did you ever tell Ms. Gardner any of this? Did she have something to hold over you? Something that might make it seem like you would want to get rid of her?"

"Of course not, I never told anybody until now. Do you think I would kill a friend to keep from going back to Jamaica?" Her voice had started to rise.

"No, but I need to understand what is out there on the internet. I am going to need to get some help from some friends of mine to clean everything up."

"But won't you have to tell them about me, won't they be able to use the information?"

"Not these particular folks. They have bigger secrets than yours and owe me some pretty substantial favors."

Beatrice closed her eyes and sighed. "I just want the lying to stop and to be left alone. Couldn't you get into trouble?'

"Trouble is my middle name." When Beatrice looked confused he laughed. "Just a joke. Don't worry about me. I have bigger secrets myself."

"What kind of secrets?"

"Um, we'll wait until I know you better to spring those on you."

They talked for a few more minutes before Lester began packing up his laptop.

"What are you going to do?"

"Well, first I'm going to go see Kestrel and tell her what we know and then I'm going to drop in on a friend of mine."

After Lester left Beatrice sat quietly for several minutes before pouring out her cold tea and pulling on her rubber gloves.

CHAPTER THIRTY-SEVEN

The Pacific Union Club, that bastion of San Francisco elitism, stood proudly on top of Nob Hill. Originally the old Flood Mansion, survivor of the 1906 earthquake, it held its place between the Fairmont Hotel on one side and Grace Cathedral on the other. For most of the wealthy it was a symbol of their belonging, and for the rest of the city, if they thought of it at all, it was a symbol of their exclusion. Not that most of them wanted to be included, although, there were some few out there who still coveted the high-cost membership and special access it gave you to what once was the "in" group in SF, but now was mostly the "old" group. Word was, they were going to run a gondola between The Towers, an elite retirement community, and the PU Club.

Kestrel worked at both of those places, not so much for the bucks, but for the access it gave her to the shenanigans of the wealthy when they thought no one was looking.

On this particular morning she'd arrived a bit early, as was usual, to check out what was going on around the club. If she'd driven to work rather than taken the bus she would have parked across the street, but she'd made her way to the Elysian Heights by public transit. She was wearing her usual uniform of black slacks, white blouse, and comfy shoes. Her frosted mane of hair had been tamed into a severe bun that hid any flashes of color; she wore non-descript, non-prescription, plain glass spectacles; and her name tag stated that she was, in fact, K. Jones. There had been a bit of a brouhaha last year about pictures being taken inside the club for that horrible gossip blog, *SFUndertheRug.com*, and now employees were required to check their cell phones in with a dour-looking matronly woman when they clocked in for their shift and retrieve them when they clocked out. Dutifully, Kestrel turned her phone off and gave it over to the woman who eyed her suspiciously. Not because she was suspicious of Kestrel, but because the lazy right eye made her look suspiciously at everyone. There was something about the turn of the head, Kestrel thought. It could make you confess to almost anything. Just not to the other phone hidden in her undergarment. Who said panty girdles were passé?

It was good that she was working today. Worrying about Beatrice and her newly discovered inheritance and being annoyed at Lester for snooping around in Beatrice's past was downright exhausting. It didn't help that she had to be so careful with her own inquiries so that her former boyfriend, Inspector Bobby Burns, wouldn't rain a torrent of hurt down on her for interfering in police business.

Once the holidays had passed and the big party season was over at the PU Club, interesting tidbits to share on the blog would be hard to come by. She had to admit that the murder of Beatrice's employer had given the site a little local color although she had to be careful about sharing any of the inside info she had.

Her good neighbor Sam was going to help her out a bit by checking with Greta Gardner's attorney to see if they could find out who else was named in the will. Her text to Bobby had gone unanswered. Beatrice swore she had not known that Greta was planning to leave her any money, and it might turn up some other more reasonable suspects.

Midmorning, her panty girdle buzzed, signaling a business call that she checked on her next trip to the ladies' room. Lester wanted to meet her for coffee between her shift at the PU Club and her dinner shift at The Towers. She usually tried to hit The Towers earlier in the day, while the old folks were more lively, but today her schedule was different.

Meeting Lester would be easy enough since, if the weather was good, she walked the few blocks between the two gigs. It just so happened that there was a coffee shop nestled snugly between them on Mason Street. She'd meet Lester there and give him a piece of her mind. She didn't care if he was a private investigator, he shouldn't be snooping around in other people's business. She did for a moment reflect on the absurdity of her annoyance considering what she did for her blog, but she dismissed it as "a totally different thing."

The lunch shift was pretty much as usual for this time of year. A few businessmen trying to impress clients with their membership, some of the members that ate here three times a week, no matter what, including her own recently discovered half-brother who carefully avoided acknowledging her. Apparently, being wealthy and having your half-sister working as the invisible staff at your club might be embarrassing. To be fair she avoided him as much as he did her. She really didn't want him blowing her cover, such as it was. One time she'd run into him outside the back entrance and he'd hissed at her. "After the pile of money you got from our family I don't understand why you insist on working here. It is bizarre, to say the least." She'd just smiled at him enigmatically and placed her index finger to her lips to signal secrecy. He'd huffed away.

The thing that Kestrel thought was strangest at the PU Club was that if a member brought a female guest to lunch they could not sit in the main dining room. It didn't really matter that much since it was all the same food from the same kitchen, but she thought it mattered to some people because she knew for a fact that many wives would not have lunch with their husbands at the club because they couldn't sit in the main dining room. Maybe that was the whole idea.

Before her shift ended she took one last trip to the loo and checked her phone. Nothing new going on so she tucked it back into its safe spot and went to clock out, smiling at the guardian of the phones when hers was handed back. She tucked the burner in the gym bag of tricks that she carried everywhere and headed for The Towers. It was a typical San Francisco winter day. Sunny, but surprisingly chilly. The temperature was not particularly low but the proximity to the bay and ocean gave it a bone-deep chill and a distinct tang in the nose and throat. You could, if desperate, park yourself against a light-colored sunlit wall to warm up, and that is exactly what many of the street people were doing. On this particular afternoon the sunny side of every street in San Francisco was lined with baskers.

She had just cleared the back parking lot, walking with her head down checking her burner phone for annoying messages from her mother and Groupon offers when she almost walked right into Bobby Burns. He remembered her habits and had placed himself exactly where he knew she would have to pass on her way whether she was going home or to The Towers.

"Whoa, Bobby. That was close. What are you doing here?"

"I'm here to see you. Why else would I be hanging around in these rarified climes?"

There had been a time when Bobby waiting to waylay her would have meant he was interested in a little afternoon delight, but she suspected that was not the case today.

"Well, walk with me then. I have a shift at The Towers and I'm meeting someone on the way."

Bobby glanced at his watch. "Okay, I just have to ask you a couple of questions."

"Ask away." Kestrel sounded more confident than she was. What had she done this time that would bring Inspector Burns to talk to her?

"Do you know a man named Sandeep Sheik?"

"Um, sounds familiar, let me think a minute." She ducked across the street between two cars stuck in the usual traffic on California Street. If you couldn't jaywalk when you were with a police officer, when could you? Actually, jaywalking wasn't really a "thing" in California since the new law went into effect. It also gave her a moment to act like she didn't know exactly who Sandeep was. "Isn't he that guy that works at the cancer center? The one that runs some of the trials?"

"Yes, that's the one. And, I have to ask, why do you know him?"

"I went there the other day with Beatrice and we talked to him for a couple of minutes."

"Why did you and Ms. Campbell go there?"

"Beatrice had a study visit for Ms. Gardner on her phone calendar and it hadn't been canceled. She didn't know if they'd been informed that Ms. Gardner would not be making that appointment."

"So, you two had to go all the way over there?"

"Beatrice just thought it would be weird to call them up and tell them that Ms. Gardner was dead. Besides, we wanted to go to a Jamaican restaurant near there and we were meeting a friend for lunch." Kestrel congratulated herself that it was all sounding very plausible.

"What happened when you got there?"

"We went up to the reception person and told her Ms. Gardner would not be coming for the appointment. When we told her why she kind of freaked out, saying it would have to be reported to someone as an adverse event or something like that. Then she said we'd need to talk to this Sandeep guy."

"Does Beatrice know him well?"

"You'll have to ask her. My feeling was that she had seen him there before but didn't really know him. He just met with Ms. Gardner at her appointments."

"So, you both talked to him. What was your impression of him?" That actually was not an unusual question for Bobby to ask Kestrel. He'd learned long ago that she had a sense for people and was a pretty good judge of character right from the get-go.

They were almost at the coffee shop and Kestrel didn't really want to introduce Bobby and Lester, so she stopped on the sidewalk. "He's good looking and he knows it. The receptionist made a remark that sort of indicated he is popular with the female patients. He gave me a smarmy feeling. Like you wanted to wash your hands when you left his office. We were only there about five minutes and then he kicked us out."

"Did he seem like he was surprised by Ms. Gardner's death?"

"I guess. I didn't think about it. What's going on with all this, Bobby?"

"I guess it is okay to tell you, the death is definitely murder, but it was set up in advance, so we're trying to determine everyone that had access to the house and who might have visited in the few weeks before the murder. Everybody's alibis for that weekend are moot. The murderer was probably not in the house when she died."

Kestrel had been fretting about the time this was taking, but that revelation stopped her train of thought in its tracks. "Did you try to contact Beatrice about this? I think she's at my place today. She didn't mention going out."

"I'm headed over that way, but I wanted to talk to you first. Do me a favor, and don't call and warn her I'm on my way."

Kestrel hesitated a moment. That had been the first thought she'd had, but, since Bobby had asked, she'd let Beatrice deal with this surprise on her own. "Only if you won't tell her you told me you were going over there."

"Deal." With that Bobby turned on his heel and headed back for Nob

Hill where he'd left his car.

CHAPTER THIRTY-EIGHT

Once Kestrel was sure Bobby was out of sight she walked the last half block to the coffee shop. She was running a few minutes late but happy to see that Lester was already there.

She'd hardly sat down at the table before she lit into him. "I want to know what is going on with Beatrice. Why are you checking her out?"

"Relax, Kestrel. I'll explain everything to you, but you need to know that I was at your place this morning talking to Beatrice. I didn't want to talk to you or do anything else until I understood what I found and got her blessing."

That took the wind out of Kestrel's sails and she sat back just as the waitress walked up to get her order. "I'll just have black coffee, thanks." She smiled at the woman.

"I was running late because Detective Burns was waiting for me outside the club. I had to shake him before I came here. Do you know him?"

"Never met the guy, but I know who he is. Homicide, right?"

"Yes, he had some questions about that guy Bea and I went to see at the cancer center." She started to tell him that Bobby was on the way to talk to Beatrice right now but was concerned he might shoot Bea a text warning her. She'd already promised Bobby that wouldn't happen. "So, tell me what is going on with Beatrice."

"First, I want you to know why I was checking her out. I am only doing what the police will be doing. I wanted to know what they would find and head off any surprises, and there are a couple of big surprises there. First, Beatrice Campbell, is not the Beatrice Campbell she claims to be."

"What? That doesn't make any sense."

"Just hold on a minute. Dang, Kestrel. Let a guy finish his story, will ya'?

"Okay, okay. Just hurry it up."

"Second, there were two Beatrice Campbells. One is…was, our Beatrice's auntie, her mother's younger sister, who was only a few years older than Bea. Beatrice number one came to the United States years ago and became a naturalized citizen in New York, working as a nanny for some high-class folks. Beatrice number two, our Beatrice, came to the United States to visit her Auntie on a temporary visa before Auntie moved to San Francisco. Auntie Beatrice was diagnosed with advanced cancer and niece Beatrice was taking care of her when they came up with a plan to allow our Beatrice to stay in the U.S. when Auntie died. Basically, they just switched identities. They were close in age and looked a lot alike. When they moved to San Francisco our Beatrice used her aunt's work history to go looking for a job in the city, which is how she hooked up with the Spencer family. She hasn't gone back to Jamaica since then for fear of running into immigration problems. Now she is petrified the authorities will find out the truth and send her back to Jamaica."

"Well, shit!" It took Kestrel a couple of minutes to process that bombshell. "Do you think the police suspect anything?"

"No, I don't, and I have a plan for making a couple of switches in some databases to make sure they don't find anything. But I needed to talk to Bea first."

"Couldn't that get you in a ton of trouble if somebody found it out?"

"Oh, yeah. But, no pain, no gain. If I can't manage this myself I have some techie friends who would consider it a challenge."

"Isn't all this really secondary to making sure Bea doesn't get charged with murder?"

"Yes, but it also eliminates a possible motive. Like, what if Greta found out and Bea killed her to keep her from squealing?"

"Beatrice wouldn't do that."

"You know that and I know that, but does Bobby Burns know that? I don't think so."

"What are you going to do to fix this?"

"I'm not telling you or Beatrice what I'm doing so you can't get blamed for anything if it doesn't work."

"What's in it for you?" Kestrel liked Lester but was a bit suspicious about his motives. Maybe he was after some of the inheritance Beatrice would get if she didn't go to prison.

Lester looked kind of sheepish. "I like Beatrice and I don't want her to go to jail or to Jamaica. I want to get a chance to know her better, no strings attached."

Considering the disparity in both height and skin tone Kestrel had trouble picturing the two of them as a couple, but then, she had trouble imagining almost any couple at home and out of the public eye. She'd made a deal with herself not to imagine those activities as soon as she'd figured out what they might entail, when she was about eleven years old and walked in on her mother with one of her boyfriends.

They'd finished their coffee and Kestrel only had a few minutes before her Towers shift started. "There's one thing I would like you to do for me. Can you see what you can find out about two people, Bertram Frankel and Annabelle Leigh? I think they were married once, to each other, I mean. I want whatever you can find, including if you need to follow them and learn what their relationship is right now. Frankel was a longtime friend of Greta Gardner and Annabelle Leigh suddenly showed up to visit Greta in the past couple of weeks."

"Sure, I can do that."

"I'm paying for this, so consider yourself on the clock. I just served them at the club and they seemed awfully chummy for exes."

"Great! By the way, did Beatrice say anything about moving into the apartment?"

"I think she's gotten a couple of job offers, but she's hoping to not have to "live in" next time. Says it's too easy to be caught up in other people's drama. She didn't say anything about the apartment but I told her I'm thinking about hiring you to clean my place."

"Very funny." Lester picked up the check for the coffee.

CHAPTER THIRTY-NINE

Beatrice was just getting into her Zen housecleaning trance when there was another knock at the door. She was on her hands and knees scraping several years of accumulated floor wax from under a cabinet and considered not answering this time. When she turned her head and peered through the legs of the table she could see that it was Bobby Burns. She figured she could just slowly back into the living room and hide until he went away but couldn't resist finding out if he had any new information.

This time she removed her gloves and headscarf before opening the door.

Inspector Burns, I'm afraid that Kestrel is at work today. In fact, I think she has two shifts and won't be home until quite late."

"I just spoke with her at the PU Club. It is you I wanted to speak with."

"Do you have any news? Any good news?"

"I have news, but it may not be good. I'm hoping you can help me figure that out."

Beatrice turned and led him into the living room. She didn't have it in her to make more undrunk tea. "Please sit down." She sat herself on the edge of the sofa and looked at him expectantly.

Bobby sat down across the small room from her. "I have been checking the security cameras at the Spencer house for the night Ms. Gardner died and it is clear that you were there the whole night, unless you climbed down the back wall and over two fences and came back the same way."

Beatrice smiled at that. "That's good news, isn't it? It means I could not have murdered her."

Bobby did not smile. "Actually, it doesn't help much because it is likely that whoever killed Ms. Gardner set up everything in advance. They likely weren't even there when she died."

"Set it up in advance? How could they do that?"

"The coroner has determined that Ms. Garnder died as the result of cyanide poisoning."

Beatrice gasped, "The champagne…?"

"No, not the champagne. She did not ingest the cyanide. It was released as a gas from items used for her bath. She actually drowned in the tub after being rendered unconscious by the cyanide gas."

"Someone poisoned her bubble bath?"

"Actually, it was likely from the bath bomb she used and the incense."

"But she'd used those things for years. How could someone know she would take a bath that night?"

"It seems that the murderer did not care exactly when she would die, only that she would eventually use the items and they would not be anywhere around when it happened. Can you tell me where Ms. Gardner obtained the bath items she used?"

"There's a store on Union Square, Lush. There are several stores in San Francisco but Greta usually sent me to pick up items at the Union Square store. Or sometimes she would just order them online. She loved online shopping. She thought it was brilliant how easy it made it to get what you wanted, whenever you wanted."

"How were the orders usually delivered? Had she had any deliveries recently, say in the past month?"

"Usually, they came within a couple of days with the mail, or by

UPS, or Fedex. They would just leave them at the front door."

"Did she buy from anyone else?"

"Someone sent her a gift basket a couple of weeks ago. It wasn't boxed up, just wrapped in cellophane and left at the door. We both thought it was odd for a store order but then decided it must be a present from someone. A surprise."

"Can you remember exactly when it was delivered?"

"Let me think. It must have been the beginning of last week, Monday I think. I had run some errands and had a lot of parcels so I parked in the driveway and came in through the front door. If I go in from the garage there is a narrow flight of steps that make carrying things difficult. The basket was sitting at the door and I just brought it in with everything else."

"Would you still have the basket and cellophane?"

"No, it would have gone out with the garbage and recycle on Thursday night to be picked up on Friday early."

Bobby's face was grim as he closed his notebook and repocketed his pen. "No chance of fingerprints, then. How about the entryway camera set-up?"

"There might still be something on that. We didn't think to try to find out who had come. I don't think it keeps the video forever, but I'm not sure how long it is available."

"Well, that's it then. We'll follow-up on the video. Of course, we'd checked it for the night she died, but hadn't thought it necessary to go back very far."

"Does this mean I'm still a suspect?"

"Everyone is still a suspect, but, unless one of your skills is handling cyanide safely, you probably didn't manufacture those poisoned items. Please let me know if you remember anything else about the delivery, or anything else, for that matter."

Beatrice walked with Bobby to the door and closed it behind him.

CHAPTER FORTY

Sunita had closed the door to her office so that she could stare unseeing into the distance without being noticed. She'd not slept well and could not focus on the stack of files on her desk and the endless list of emails that grew longer every second. She did not care about the quarterly reports or any of the demands being made on her time and energy. She cared only about the call she'd received last night from Sandeep.

She was dead, the woman who had stood in the way of her marriage was gone. Greta Gardner: she'd never actually met the woman, but she'd symbolized everything that was missing in Sunita's life. Her mood swung between elation over the possibilities and fear. What new obstacle would Sandeep come up with to prevent their marriage?

After a few minutes she became aware of raised voices in the outer office: A woman's strident demands and the reconciling murmur of her staffer in response. She tried to ignore them but finally stood and walked to the door.

Pasting on her patient and caring visage she opened the door and stepped out into a seeming standoff between her frustrated assistant and an older woman.

"I am very sorry Ms. Leigh, but we have no record of your transfer of insurance and change of address in our system." Mary was trying very hard to keep her voice conciliatory and suitably respectful, but Sunita could hear the edge in it.

"That is not my problem. I moved back to the area recently and now I need to see a doctor and my records have not been transferred."

"Yes, I can see that, but it is another department, the Patient Records Department, that would have received your change of address and requested your former medical group to forward them. When did you make the change? Getting those files transferred can sometimes take several weeks."

"I don't recall when I contacted you people, but I can see no reason why my information is not here."

"Perhaps you could go to the Records department and check with them, I can call and let them know you are on your way." Mary's hand was already on the telephone receiver in anticipation of moving this problem on to someone else, anyone else.

"I am certainly not going to run around all over this hospital trying to get this straightened out. I insist you call the other department and find out who screwed this up."

Sunita suspected that the person who screwed this up was standing there in front of Mary's desk, dressed in expensive clothes, and looking haughty. Sunita took a deep breath, pasted on her most dazzling smile, and stepped forward. "Good morning, I am Ms. Khan, the Finance Manager, perhaps I can be of help." She automatically reached out for a handshake greeting.

The older woman looked at her outstretched hand in disdain and ignored the invitation. "Finally, someone who can resolve this issue." Annabelle gazed at Sunita for a moment. "Haven't we met before?"

"I don't imagine that we have unless you have been in this office before. I understand you are new to the area."

"Yes, I've recently returned to San Francisco, but, I am sure we have met. I am very good with faces, but not always names."

The woman did look slightly familiar to Sunita and she thought quickly to place it before a chill ran up her spine. For a moment the smile on her face dimmed. "I have a very common face; I am sure I would have recalled meeting someone as distinguished as yourself."

The flattery allayed Annabelle's suspicious expression but only for a moment. "No, I am positive it was you. But no worries, I am sure to recall exactly where and when. I always do. In the meantime, what are you going to do about getting my records straightened out?"

Sunita wanted to say something like, "I am going to kick your entitled bum out of my office and get on with my day," but she did not. She turned to Mary who'd been standing with her arms akimbo waiting for the slap-down she expected Sunita to come up with. Her boss was eminently professional, but did not suffer fools gladly, so she was surprised when Sunita said, "Mary, why don't you take your break now and go get a nice cup of tea. I will take care of this."

"I would love a cup of tea myself, milk, two sugars," Annabelle chimed in.

Mary bristled but Sunita placed a calming hand on her arm as she reached into her own pocket and drew out her staff card. "Why don't you take my card to the cafeteria and get some lovely drinks for all of us, at my expense. Ask the other ladies what they would like. I will take Ms.... I'm sorry, what is your name again?" She turned to Annabelle.

"Ms. Leigh, Annabelle Leigh."

"Yes, of course. I will take Ms. Leigh into my office and see if I can resolve her issue and the rest of you can have a little break. Ms. Leigh and I will take our tea in my office. Get some cookies and pastries, as well. We might as well make a party of it."

If Mary was shocked at her boss's suggestion she hid it well. Sunita had not been herself lately and this was just another evidence of that. She took the card and went about getting drink orders from the other two staff members who did not try to hide their surprise but were quick to order their favorite drinks and snacks before the offer could be withdrawn.

Sunita turned back to her office and motioned Annabelle ahead of her. She felt some solace for the affront to her position in that most certainly Ms. Leigh's tea would not be delivered unadulterated in some harmless but nasty way.

Seated in her office with the door firmly closed Sunita turned to her computer. "Could you please spell your name for me?"

"Certainly, A-N-N-A-B-E-L-L-E L-E-I-G-H."

"And I will need your Social Security number and birth date to access your records." Sunita typed the information into the computer and scanned the screen. "I see that you were seen at the medical center a number of times some years ago. It shows your address as 417 Vallejo Street. Is that still correct?"

"No, I moved from San Francisco to the East Coast long ago and have only now returned. I am renting a temporary place at 1847 Fulton Street, near Alamo Square."

"All right, I am inserting that address. Do you have a phone number where you can be reached, and a current e-mail?"

Annabelle gave her cell phone number. "How long is this going to take? I need to get some prescriptions refilled before long."

Ignoring the question, Sunita asked "What is the name of your former doctor?"

"Dr. Kendall on Peachtree Street in Orlando."

Sunita was confident Annabelle did not know the address and would bridle at any more questions. She would look up the information and send an expedited request to Records to obtain the transfer. In her heart she knew that Annabelle had never requested that they be sent and was making a fuss over her own lack of preparation.

By the time that Sunita had looked up Dr. Kendall and sent a special email to Marilyn in Records, Mary had returned with the drinks and Annabelle was ready to depart. Sunita did not miss the self-satisfied Cheshire Cat smile the older woman gave Mary. It was unfortunate that Ms. Leigh would not be staying to drink the tea that had been delivered. Sunita could only hope that her own beverage had not been tampered with.

When Annabelle had departed and Sunita was again alone in her office, she eyed her drink before dumping it into the wastebasket. Even docile Mary could only be pushed so far.

Sunita was a person who loved a plan and had been at a loss about how to proceed when her last plan had been successfully completed. She knew exactly where Annabelle Leigh remembered her from, and that would need to be taken care of as soon as possible, before the woman could recall the circumstances.

The murmur of voices in the outer office was muffled with the munching of cookies and swilling of elaborate barista drinks. The cost was certainly worth it.

CHAPTER FORTY-ONE

Annabelle hurriedly gathered up her belongings for today's outing. The extended call from Bertie had her running late and she had a long list of things to do.

First, the medical center had called that her prescriptions were ready and there were papers to sign. It was annoying to have to go back there, but the head of finance had called her personally. At least that Indian woman took her seriously and gave her the respect she deserved. She wished she could remember where she had seen her before but knew it would come to her eventually. She'd found that chasing a memory around her aging brain was usually futile and it was better to wait until the sought knowledge just popped into her consciousness. Among her Florida friends she'd been notorious for texting them two days later in the middle of the night with the name, or word, or reference she'd struggled with at lunch on Wednesday.

She'd decided to Uber around the city today rather than take her chances on finding parking places. It had been the same when she'd lived in NYC. It just wasn't worth it to keep a car anymore.

She grabbed up papers, reading glasses, a bottle of water, a light sweater in case the weather got cooler and a hat in case the weather got warmer. Everything got stuffed into her over-sized bag, Gucci of course.

Bertie's call had flustered her. Greta's recent death had been a shock, and now the police had been asking him questions about Greta's will and why he was included in it. He'd never mentioned that Greta would be leaving him money, so now it looked suspicious since it was common knowledge in certain circles that he was living on the edge of his fortune. She just couldn't think about it now. She'd arranged to meet him for dinner and they could discuss it then. One of her stops was Greta's attorney's office. She wanted to get a handle on the plans for the house and get a bid in before it went public. Moving into the place would cement her revenge on her old frenemy, as well as get her out of this less-than-perfect condo. San Francisco was not the city she remembered it being, and slogging her way through homeless encampments and beggars' enclaves was not how she wanted to spend her day.

She checked her phone when she reached the lobby. Her Uber was still a few minutes away; she might as well stand on the curb to wait and hope she didn't get accosted too many times for cash.

The sky was gray and a light mist was falling. Unfortunately, the one thing she hadn't stuffed into her capacious bag was the nifty portable umbrella she'd recently bought.

As she stepped to the curb and glanced hurriedly around to see if she could spot her ride—they'd said a black Toyota Corolla—her phone rang.

She dug in her bag and pulled out the phone, focused completely on that one thing. It was an unknown number and as she pushed the answer button and raised the phone to her ear she looked into the face of the driver of a car that had just sped up to jump the curb and send her flying across the sidewalk and into the wall of the building.

Annabelle Leigh remembered nothing of the event, but bystanders reported the automobile reversing and driving over her inert body a second time before swerving back onto the street and speeding away. The license numbers had been obscured and the driver wore dark glasses and a hooded sweatshirt. It had all happened so fast that witnesses would have thought it was a tragic accident if the car hadn't reversed and run her over a second time.

Inspector Bobby Burns would not normally have been at the hospital for a traffic accident, even a seemingly intentional one, unless the victim were dead and murder was suspected. In this case he'd been called in because the victim had a connection to the homicide he was investigating.

He'd been briefed by the officer, who had conducted interviews at the site, and the contents of Ms. Leigh's bag were currently spread out across the empty bed in the room.

The phone had been thrown clear in the impact and the screen was badly cracked, but it seemed to be in working order. The crime scene folks would have to work with the provider and the phone to open her call history, but as he sifted through the papers the phone began to ring. Glancing at it he saw the name and smiling face of another of his favorite suspects come up on the damaged screen. Bertie Frankel. Bobby figured the victim's ex-husband was a good place to start.

"Mr. Frankel, this is Inspector Burns, of the SFPD. I see that you are trying to contact Ms. Annabelle Leigh."

There was silence on the line until a wavering voice responded. "Inspector Burns, what's happened to Annabelle?"

Before Bobby could answer the voice took on a more urgent tone. "Wait a minute, you are Homicide. Oh my god, Annabelle isn't dead, is she?"

"No, Mr. Frankel, Ms. Leigh is not dead, but she has been badly injured in a suspicious automobile incident and is currently hospitalized."

"Where are you...where is she?" The voice seemed calmer.

"She has been admitted to UC Hospital on Sutter and I am with her, trying to determine what happened and whether it has any bearing on my case."

"Your case? You mean Greta's murder? How could it have anything to do with that? Annabelle had nothing to do with that."

"I am not saying she did, Mr. Frankel. We always investigate coincidental events."

"Well, can I come to the hospital to see her?"

"That will be up to her doctors. At this point she is unconscious, but I am sure she would appreciate you coming down. Fortunately, I will still be here and we will have an opportunity to chat."

"Okay, well, I'll come over then." Mr. Frankel didn't sound very enthusiastic about talking to Bobby, but he could hardly back down now.

While Bobby waited for Bertie to arrive he glanced at the documents from the bag. The most interesting pieces were the printouts of information on the house on Walnut Street, so recently occupied by Greta Gardner.

Luckily for Bobby, older folks still kept calendars or diaries on paper as well as on their phones and Annabelle's included her activities for the day: pick up prescriptions and paperwork at UCSF, an appointment with an attorney, oddly enough, Greta Gardner's attorney, a nail appointment complete with facial, and finally, a dinner with Bertie at the Pacific Union Club.

Bobby and Rocky would be having dinner together as well, but nothing as fancy as the PU Club. She'd sent him a text saying that her latest Fraud investigation had gone sideways and he'd offered to bring pizza and beer to her place as consolation.

When Bertie arrived, fastidiously dressed, and much calmer than he'd sounded on the phone, Bobby escorted him to the hospital cafeteria and talked to him over a cup of coffee.

"I'm sorry that your friend has been injured, Mr. Frankel."

"Annabelle is much more than a friend; she is my wife…my ex-wife, and we were hoping to re-establish our relationship. And just call me Bertie, Mr. Frankel was my father."

"Reconciliation isn't always an easy thing to do, I've heard."

"Well, we're older and wiser now. Some of the things that were deal-breakers twenty years ago just don't seem so important now."

"Well, I hope she recovers soon." Bobby almost said, "I hope she recovers." But softened it a bit in the end. From what he'd seen and heard from the staff, her recovery was not a given as her injuries were major and it would be touch-and-go for a while.

"Tell me, Bertie, do you own a car?"

"No, I don't. Of course, I do know how to drive, but it's expensive and difficult to keep a car in San Francisco."

"How do you get around, then?

"I used to have a car and driver but that doesn't make much sense either. I used to use taxis a lot, but now I use Uber or Lyft. That's how I got here today."

"I believe Ms. Leigh was waiting for an Uber when the accident occurred. Do you know what her plans were today?"

"I knew some of them. We had talked on the phone right before she went out today. She had some appointments and we were going to have dinner together. She indicated there might be something to celebrate."

Bobby wondered if the celebration had anything to do with the money Bertie would be receiving from Greta's estate or if it had something to do with the real estate information on Greta's house. Either way it seemed at least tenuously related to his murder investigation.

CHAPTER FORTY-TWO

Bobby was looking forward to a quiet evening with Rocky. He shifted the pizza box, six-pack of brews, and perfectly chilled bottle of Sauvignon Blanc to awkwardly knock on her apartment door.

It was becoming more and more comfortable for them to spend an evening talking rather than going out. Out was just too people-y. Her apartment: quieter, soothingly decorated, and calm, was the best medicine for him after a frustrating day like he'd just had.

"Christ, why can't I get a handle on this case?" he'd muttered to himself as the elevator brought him to Rocky's floor. There were too many suspects, and none at all, it seemed. Greta Gardner hadn't seemed to have a lot of enemies, but there were a few people who would benefit from her death. Bobby knew that everyone had their secrets, as well. Had Greta known something someone was anxious to keep hidden?

He heard the click of the deadbolt and the door swung open. It looked like Rocky had gotten home a bit early and managed to take a quick shower. Her hair was piled up on her head and she was wearing those gauzy pants and loose top that made her look so tall and cool.

The door opened wider and he could see beyond her into her apartment. The wide windows revealed the darkened sky outside and the warm lamplight of the room.

"Perfect timing," she smiled as she reached out to take the bottle of wine and beers from him.

"We aim to please."

"What's in the box? It smells wonderful."

"Just Papa Gianni's meatball special with extra mushrooms."

"Yum. I am starving. Frustration gives me the munchies."

"You and me, both." Bobby followed her into the apartment and set the warm box on the kitchen counter. "I was hoping you'd be having more success than I am this week." He popped open the pizza box.

Rocky pulled a couple of plates and a wineglass from the cabinet and swooped in to grab a piece of the fragrant pie. "Well, we're close on this guy, but it takes so long to get the data all together and build a case. The forensic accountant has been pulling out what little there is of his hair, all week. We know where the money comes from and how he gets it, but it is hard to prove that what he is doing with it is illegal."

Bobby helped himself to the biggest slice of pie that he could find and opened one of the beers. "You said he gets sick women to leave him money. Isn't that illegal?"

Rocky had poured a healthy dose of the wine into her glass and settled at the table. "It isn't illegal to get people to leave you money, but he's set up some phony foundation that sounds like it's a non-profit for some benefit to somebody, somewhere. It might be legit, but he's not filing taxes on it and there doesn't seem to be anyone else attached except for some friend of his from the university. Someone in finance who's squeaky clean as near as we can tell."

"Well, at least you don't have a dead body waiting for some justice."

"There are a number of dead people, but none that were murdered, as far as I know."

For several minutes the only sounds in the apartment were the appreciative sighs and quiet chewing. Both Bobby and Rocky were enthusiastic eaters. Neither one of them cared much about cooking, but they were savvy critics of other people's efforts.

There was not a lot left of the meal when they finally pushed back from the table. Bobby was covetously eying the last two slices and wondering how ungallant it would be to claim them for tomorrow's breakfast. That hope was put to rest when Rocky quickly wrapped them in foil and stowed them in the fridge; she was a fan of cold pizza for breakfast, as well. "Do you want another beer?" she offered.

"Sure." He guessed he'd have to settle for that.

Bobby removed himself to the comfy couch and Rocky sat back down resting her elbows on the table and her chin in her hands.

With full bellies and a little alcohol buzzing through their veins they could both just let their minds wander.

Bobby stirred himself to look at Rocky. "So, how does this guy get the women to leave him money when they die?"

Rocky stood up and walked to the couch, turning on a lamp as she passed. "We don't know, exactly. It doesn't seem like it's a romantic thing. They are much older and very ill when he first meets them."

"Like meeting through friends or at a club or something?"

"No, he meets them at a cancer center, they're all elderly women patients with breast cancer."

"You're kidding. At UCSF in the Cancer Center?"

"Yes, that's where he works. I hear he can be quite charming, though I didn't see it. He obviously didn't want to be talking to me."

Bobby sat upright. "What's this dude's name?"

"Sheik, Sandeep Sheik. Why?"

"Because my vic, Greta Gardner, was being treated at the Cancer Center and that Sandeep guy was her coordinator, or something. She was in a clinical trial."

"Holy shit." Rocky moved to the couch.

"Okay, let's not jump to conclusions. I'll tell you mine and you tell me yours, and we'll see if they jibe."

"Me first." Rocky sat back and took a deep breath, gathering her thoughts. "This guy we're investigating works at UCSF at the Cancer Center, running clinical trials, mostly breast cancer studies. The women are enrolled in the studies because the usual treatments have failed and it is their last hope. Sometimes they live a little longer, if the treatment is working, but eventually they die. Over the course of the past two or three years our department has been contacted by the families of these women who have noticed that they bequeathed rather large chunks of money to a non-profit foundation called Shining Hope. The families wanted us to find out what the foundation was and who was running it. We went through the legal and financial records of all the women treated at the center who had died in the past two years and found that many of the wealthy ones, without much family, had left money to Shining Hope. Most recently we were able to go back through several layers of legal maneuvers and found out that the non-profit was started by Sandeep Sheik and a woman named Sunita Khan. Sheik is a doctor in India, but not licensed here. What we haven't been able to find out is where the money goes, whether it's a legitimate foundation."

"All right, my turn then. My victim, Greta Gardner, was an older, wealthy woman, with no family to speak of. Most of her money was left to charities of different kinds, but she had recently changed her will to benefit an old friend, a caregiver, and the Shining Hope Foundation. We've been looking at the caregiver and the old friend and his ex-wife but had no reason to question the foundation. That opens a whole new can of worms."

"So, Sandeep Sheik knew your victim?"

"He definitely knew her, but there's nothing to say they had contact outside the hospital. No one has mentioned seeing him at her house or any place else. Kestrel said she had been getting better on the trial."

"Kestrel! What does she have to do with this?"

"She's a friend of the caregiver, Beatrice Campbell. They went to the cancer center to talk to this guy after Greta died."

Rocky did not look happy. "The last thing in the world we need is Kestrel Jonas poking her little busybody nose into this investigation."

"She's not, I already told her to back off. She's just concerned about her friend."

"Yeah, right. I don't trust her, Bobby. She's either up to something or going to mess things up digging around."

Bobby knew there was no point in arguing with Rocky. She was never going to be a fan of Kestrel's, not least because she was one of his ex-girlfriends and had solved a murder out from under Rocky when she was in Homicide. "Did anyone ever tell you that you are very sexy when you are solving crimes?"

Rocky smiled. "Not lately. So, what do we do now?"

"Well, I can think of a few things, but most of them can't be done until Monday, so I vote for watching a little television and seeing where it leads us." With that he picked up the remote and they both cuddled down into the sofa.

CHAPTER FORTY-THREE

Sandeep was not normally a nervous person. It surprised him that he had felt jumpy and anxious all day and now that the time for the call with his parents drew nearer, he found he couldn't settle. He took out the envelope he'd received again and rifled through the papers inside it.

He did not need to review the photographs again. He'd already determined that the young woman was attractive enough. She was healthy, not too dark skinned, a little stern looking, but those things mattered little to him. What did hold his interest was the extensive information about her family, education, background, and maybe most important, the extensive financial holdings of her parents. She was already practicing medicine in the United States, and her family was anxious for her to make a match with another physician and were willing to finance and support him completing his credentials in the states and later set him and this new wife in a private practice. Something he would never be able to do on his own.

He could tell that his parents, especially his mother, had taken a hand in assuring that his marriage would benefit his entire family.

This was not the first envelope of this type he had received from his mother. Periodically a thick packet of materials and photos would arrive for him to review, but this one was the first he'd been really excited about. He was more anxious now to marry, as his plan had not gone the way he'd hoped when he moved to San Francisco. Some of the other women had been more attractive, many had been as wealthy, but some had huge families to share the wealth. This woman was not too attractive, less so than he was. She would be happy to marry someone so good looking and charming. She had no siblings to share the money. In many ways he would be lucky to make such a match, but he would never let on that was the case. He knew that she had received a similar package of information about him, and he suspected that there had already been approval to proceed from her side.

Tonight, he would have the teleconference with his parents, and they would discuss the details of the marriage agreement. They would talk about arrangements for him to speak with her, and before long, for them to meet. His parents would travel to meet with her family in India. Elaborate plans would be made for a huge wedding in Mumbai, where her family lived, and he would begin the costly and complicated process of becoming a licensed physician in Chicago, where she lived.

He would not be sorry to leave San Francisco. It had not turned out to be the answer to his dreams and he could already envision the successful, and well deserved, life that he would have with the wife his mother had found for him.

The call with his parents did not take long. It was more a business meeting than a family chat. Of course, his mother was thrilled that he was pursuing marriage. She assured him he could leave everything to her, she would take care of it all.

He was deep in revery thinking about what the future held when his phone rang. It was Sunita. He let it ring a couple of times before picking it up. He hadn't given any thought to her at all during the evening, but he knew that he would need to tell her about his bride, if only so that he could explain gathering his various belongings and removing them from her apartment.

Finally, he picked up his phone. "Hello Sunita."

"Hello, Sandeep. I am sorry to call so late, but I wondered if you would like to come for dinner tomorrow night."

He hesitated for a moment, "Sure, I could come for dinner tomorrow." He might as well get this over with. "We can have a bit of a celebration. I have some exciting news."

"Really, I can't wait to hear what it is. I will make something special."

"Lovely. I can be there about 7:00. Will that work for you?"

"Yes, that is perfect. See you then. Sleep well."

"Goodnight." Sandeep found that he was excited to tell Sunita his plans. He realized she would be disappointed, but surely she couldn't have seriously expected him to marry her. They were just friends. In fact, she was the only friend he had to share the news with. She would see the sense of it. If nothing else, Sunita was practical.

CHAPTER FORTY-FOUR

Sunita had planned carefully for this dinner with Sandeep. She knew that both his roommates were away this weekend, some sports league they belonged to. And she knew that Sandeep would be sitting alone bemoaning the fact that he would have to conjure up his own meal for the evening. He might even regret breaking up with her if only because she always made him dinner on Friday nights.

She had not slept well and had not bothered to apply her usual careful makeup. Since his visit to her apartment last night, she had played and replayed the scene in her head until she thought she would scream. She'd been stricken, and then furious.

"My family has finally arranged an appropriate marriage for me, another doctor here in the States. She is eminently suitable, and now that I will be receiving money for the foundation, I can afford to marry." He'd acted excited at the news, and then surprised that she didn't see the obvious. "A marriage with you could not possibly have been considered.

Surely, you see that." If he felt any regret for having dangled marriage before her, he did not show it.

Of course, she had not seen that, at all, and made a perfect fool of herself, crying, begging, and threatening, all to no avail. Sandeep always hated a scene and he only glanced back pityingly as he left her sobbing on the floor and closed the door behind him.

The dark entrance and isolated aspect of his home suited her purposes. She rang the bell and then knocked when he did not answer. She could hear the rustle of someone against the door, peering through the peephole. "Sandeep, it's just me. I wanted to bring you some food and say a proper good-bye."

The door opened a bit and revealed him eyeing her through the crack.

"It is no good, Sunita. We are not destined to marry."

"Yes, you are right. You have much better opportunities ahead of you, especially now that you will be receiving money from your dear friend." She raised the bottle of champagne before him and smiled. "There is no reason we cannot part as friends. I don't want things to end on the ugly scene from last night."

His eyes lowered to the carry-out bag at her feet. The aroma of chicken tikka masala and fresh naan bread scented the air.

Finally, he stepped back and swung the door open, then turned and strode back into the shabby apartment.

"I brought food from Amber India instead of cooking tonight. No chance of me poisoning you." They both laughed.

Sandeep had disappeared into the kitchen and returned with a couple of plates and forks. "I don't have any fancy glasses for the wine."

"No problem, I brought my own."

Sandeep opened each of the containers and deeply inhaled the spicy smells from his favorite restaurant. When he had piled his plate high, he sat at the dining table. "Aren't you going to have any?"

"Yes, of course, I was just letting you serve yourself first." Sunita picked up a plate and served herself some of the basmati rice, spicy chicken, and warm naan bread before she sat down across the table from him.

She had placed the bottle of champagne in the middle of the table. "Can you open the wine for me? I'd love for us to make a toast to your new ventures."

As he opened the bottle with a muffled pop, she began to eat the food before her, then she pulled two glasses from her large purse and took the bottle from him. "Let me pour for us so that you can start eating before your food gets cold."

Sandeep obediently sat down and began to eat, his attention fully focused on his heaping plate.

Sunita placed one of the filled glasses in front of him and raised her own in a toast. "Here's to your promising future, Dr. Sheik."

He picked up his glass and drank deeply. She had counted on him swilling down the bubbly drink the same way he did his beers, and that is exactly what he did.

She drank, too, and watched him over the rim of her glass as his attention reverted to his food.

It didn't take long for him to drop his fork and clutch his throat. His looked at her and his eyes widened at the triumphant grin on her face.

"Oh, poor Sandeep. Did something you ate not agree with you?"

He glanced at her half-empty plate and then quickly to the wine bottle and her half-full glass.

"Oh, don't worry, dear. I am fine, only you will die tonight."

He looked around frantically for the cell phone that he'd left on the counter and she pulled it from her pocket.

"Sorry, but you won't be making any calls tonight, either."

He stood and immediately collapsed onto the floor. She could see that he was not yet dead, so she leaned over him and spoke rapidly before he could lose consciousness.

"Dear Sandeep. Now that you were going to get your money, thanks to me, you thought you could dump me and go on with your life. But that's not how this will end. Yes, I killed the old woman because I thought you would marry me, but you've made it very clear that is never going to happen, so now I have killed you, as well."

The man at her feet rolled onto his side and vomited.

"You would be surprised how easy it is to kill again once you have done it. Now there is just one more person for me to get rid of."

When Sandeep had stopped writhing at her feet Sunita rose and methodically rinsed the dishes, started the dishwasher, and picked up the remains of the food and champagne, as well as her champagne flutes. She wiped her fingerprints from his phone, took the remaining food and champagne bottle.

She made a final tour of the apartment, especially his bedroom, to ensure there were no pictures of her or other evidence that she even existed in his consciousness. But, of course, there were none.

On his dresser an embossed file folder lay open to the picture of his bride. Pretty, she thought, but a bit aggressive looking around the eyes. She might have saved him from a sad fate, after all.

After a moment she closed the folder and slipped it into her bag, as well.

That had gone surprisingly well. Now she just needed to get rid of one more person and she would be able to pick up her plans where they had derailed. She had always been very efficient.

CHAPTER FORTY-FIVE

Kestrel was enjoying her rare morning of leisure and solitude. She'd almost forgotten what it was like to have a roommate. Beatrice was a friend, and a sweet person, besides which she was a compulsive cleaner, and Kestrel's duplex had never been so clean and tidy. Still, there always seemed to be somebody there, sometimes multiple somebodies. Much of the time Beatrice and Lester were hanging out. They didn't take up all that much space, but people just expected you to talk to them, or else they were talking to you, or scrolling through their phones with the volume up, or streaming something on the TV. Kestrel had a TV, of course. In fact, it was a pretty big, smart TV (what else was she supposed to do with the money she'd inherited?), but she almost never watched it when she was alone. Of course, her phone was another thing. She wasn't a complete Luddite, but she did usually keep the volume down. Even she didn't want to hear all that nonsense.

A couple of times Beatrice had brought her former nanny charges,

Lisbeth and Lucy Spencer, over on one of their outings. Usually, their outings were framed around teaching the girls something useful, but Kestrel didn't know what hanging around her apartment was supposed to teach them. Maybe what they didn't want to be when they grew up.

Today it was blissfully quiet. She'd stayed in bed late, brought her coffee back with her while she worked with her laptop propped on her knees, and had just sent the latest issue of *SFUndertheRug.com* into the multi-verse.

During the COVID lockdown her blog had really taken off. Both her readers and her subjects were stuck at home and anxious for some excitement. Even she had been shocked at how much mischief the idle rich had been able to get up to in the midst of a plague. She'd read Defoe's *Journal of the Plague Year* and noted that people hadn't changed much in the 350 years since the bubonic plague ravaged London.

Her usual "army of minions," as Bobby liked to call them, had been restricted at first with the closing of restaurants and bars. The clubs and vendors who usually paid to advertise with her pulled back in confusion when they had to limit their service to online shopping and pick-up/delivery options. But, always resourceful, people had found ways to sell their wares, and online links worked perfectly on the website.

Of course, now that things had opened up and people felt free again to flaunt their money and privilege, they just let their freak flags fly.

When she heard a knock at her door she seriously considered just pretending she wasn't home, but it was beyond her to do that unless it was her mother or the police at the door, and she didn't expect either of them today.

When she peeked through the curtains on the door she was surprised that it was the police, after all, although it didn't look like an official visit.

Rocky stood looking away from the door, dressed in jeans, a large T-shirt, and running shoes. She bounced on her feet nervously and it looked like she was about to sprint away when Kestrel swung open the door.

"Rocky, wow, what a surprise."

"Yeah, well, you're not as surprised as I am." The woman smiled ruefully.

"Come on in. What can I do for you? I don't think I've been doing anything illegal lately, unless it's about those unpaid parking fines…"

"Nah, Fraud doesn't really care where you park." Rocky entered the kitchen and glanced around. "Not much has changed since I was last here."

"Well, you aren't investigating me as a possible murderer this time, I hope."

"Nope, not in Homicide, anymore. Kill whoever you like."

"Thanks, I'm good, although my mother might be in trouble. Sit down, I'll make us some coffee."

The tall woman pulled out one of the kitchen chairs and sat.

Kestrel had pulled open the cabinet for cups but turned back to her guest. "You know, it's after noon, we could have wine, unless this visit is official."

Rocky hesitated; she'd heard about Kestrel's undiscriminating palate when it came to wine but decided to go on faith. "Wine would be great." This wasn't going to be an easy conversation.

With generously poured, not too cheap, white wine in front of them, the two women looked at each other across the table.

Kestrel resisted the urge to fill the silence as they sipped their wine and the other woman glanced around the room, avoiding eye contact. One thing Kestrel had learned was not to jump the gun when someone wanted to talk but didn't want to say anything.

Finally, Rocky spoke. "Look, I don't even know why I came here, except that I don't have many women friends, and you know Bobby, and all."

"Yes, I am a woman and I do know Bobby, so if those are the requirements for what you want to talk about, you've got the right girl."

Rocky heaved a big sigh and started again. "Bobby is a really nice guy, solid, a good man."

"Agreed, but…"

"No buts, he's great, but he wants to meet my family."

"And they are not great?"

"No, that's not it. They're great, too."

"So, he's great, they're great…what's the problem?"

Rocky closed her eyes for a moment. When they opened there were tears in them. "I just don't know if they will agree each other is great."

Kestrel didn't really know what to say. Many times, she'd shied away from introducing boyfriends to her mother, so she kind of understood some of what Rocky might be feeling.

"I didn't grow up like Bobby, in the suburbs, with two parents and Little League, and summer trips to Disneyland. My mom was, is, great, but there were a bunch of us and we lived in the projects. Some of us got in trouble; dumb stuff, shoplifting, drinking, but my mother was fierce and she set us straight and now everyone is doing good. Making a living, raising babies, getting by."

"Bobby isn't going to care about any of that stuff. He's a cop, he's seen it all."

"I know that, but I think my family will look at him like a cop and not just a nice man."

"But you're a cop."

"Yeah, I know." Rocky stayed silent again for a few moments. "That wasn't easy for them, either. They accepted it because they love me but they don't really understand it."

Kestrel remained silent and took another swig of wine.

"Bobby is serious about me, about us. He wants us to move in together. He's been talking about the East Bay to be closer to my family. I don't know how to handle this."

"Have you talked to your mom or any of your family about Bobby?"

"Not really, I never know how to bring it up."

"Well, I think you should start off by breaking the news to your family. Maybe mention you've met someone, that he's white, that he's a cop, that you like him a lot. Pick the person you think will be most accepting and most wants you to be happy."

"My mom, I guess. She'd probably be glad I met someone; she worries about me being alone."

"That's a good start. I wouldn't spring him on everyone at the family picnic or anything, just get some folks on your side to start with. Um, and I would mention what you're thinking to Bobby, so he knows what's going on." Kestrel didn't mention the earlier call from Bobby. No point in raising any issues.

They chatted a bit and finished their wine, but eventually, Rocky stood up to leave. "I don't know why I came here for advice. It's not like you exactly have a great relationship going."

"Thanks for noticing. You know, it is possible to know the right things to do without ever doing them. It's a gift."

They both smiled and walked out onto the porch together. Kestrel stood for a few minutes watching Rocky's car out of sight. "It's a gift," she repeated to herself as she turned and went back through the door.

CHAPTER FORTY-SIX

The caravan of vehicles that escorted Annabelle from the hospital to her apartment on Fulton Street could have used an official escort of its own. Leading the way was the specially hired ambulance, followed by a dark-windowed Tesla driven by Dr. Chandon and carrying Bertie, then Bobby Burns's muscle car, left over from his younger days, and finally the faded, ancient VW Bug driven by Kestrel and carrying Beatrice to the destination of her new care assignment.

Of course, there was no parking on the street, and everyone double-parked along the front of the elegant building, each assured of their privilege and rank; ambulance, doctor, policeman, caregiver… It was a San Francisco thing.

Annabelle was delivered to her door on a gurney. She had been released from the hospital rather quickly, because her injuries were less extensive than first thought, and that's how hospitals do things these days. Of course, not everyone had the entitled services of one of San

Francisco's concierge doctors who was on call to see her whenever he was needed. The $5,000 a year that she paid to assure he was at her beck and call was nothing to her. However, even Dr. Chandon had been cautious enough to ensure that Beatrice was appropriately trained to assist Annabelle in her recovery. He was always available and a visiting nurse would be coming by every day for any assistance that required medical training. While the SFPD hadn't approved an ongoing police presence for security, officers would be checking in and Beatrice had been briefed on how to handle calls and visitors. Bobby couldn't be sure that this "accident" was connected to Greta's murder, or just some wackadoodle SF driver. If bystanders hadn't insisted the car was occupied, he'd have wondered if it wasn't one of those driverless cars he'd been reading about.

A service had been dispatched to the condo earlier to provide all the special equipment needed. A hospital bed, bedside toilet, pumps, meters, and gauges; the things that go bump, chirp, beep, and ding in the night.

It took some time for the hubbub to subside and by the time Annabelle and Beatrice were alone in the apartment—meds taken, dinner ordered, cautions reiterated—Beatrice was already finding out that taking care of Annabelle Leigh was a very different job than taking care of Greta Gardner had been.

"Oh, Beatrice, dear, could you please get me a glass of ice water?"

Beatrice stepped to the bedside stand and picked up the pitcher of water.

"Not that water, it's gone too cold, I think. I'd like a glass of filtered water from the door of the fridge and three ice cubes."

"Three ice cubes?"

"Yes, I want it to be cold, but not too cold."

"Okay, Ms. Leigh. I'll be right back."

In the kitchen Beatrice was careful to count out the specified three ice cubes before returning to the living room where the hospital bed had been installed.

"Thank you, dear." Annabelle took a sip of the water and winced, slightly. "Actually, do you think you could get me one more fresh ice cube? This is not quite cold enough."

"Sure. Why don't I bring a little dish with a few more cubes?"

"Oh, that would be wonderful."

When Beatrice returned from the kitchen Annabelle added a cube, took a single sip, sighed contentedly, and set the glass aside. "I'm so glad the doctor said I could recuperate from my accident at home. I am really just kind of banged up other than the head injury. A concussion I guess. I don't seem to be able to remember exactly what happened. I just remember waking up in the hospital feeling like holy hell."

"I can imagine you felt pretty beat up. I understand it is harder to recover from a fall as you get older."

Annabelle pulled a face as she considered the "getting older" reference, but let it go for now. "Yes, I've actually had worse horseback and skiing accidents back in the day."

"I've never ridden a horse or skied, so I haven't experienced that."

"Oh, my dear, we must get you out into the world."

The doorbell rang and Beatrice let the conversation drop at that and went to answer the door. Saved by the food delivery.

By the time Annabelle had thoroughly demolished her dinner, complaining non-stop that it was cold, unseasoned, unappealing, and generally not up to her usual standard, Beatrice had picked up the room a bit and moved her own meal into the kitchen where she could zap it in the microwave and eat in peace. It was going to be a long few weeks.

Bobby had received the call on Sunday night that Sandeep Sheik had been found dead by his roommates when they returned from their weekend outing.

Shit, he hated it when his prime suspect in a murder was murdered himself. Rocky hadn't been too thrilled to have her perpetrator out of the picture, either. At least, he was probably the bad guy in her crime. Unfortunately, he'd just escaped the long arm of the law by being swept up by a bigger and more undeniable arm.

They had agreed to meet at Sandeep's crime-scene apartment when Bobby had finished escorting Ms. Leigh and the gang to her lodgings. After listening to her complain for twenty minutes he was grateful that he wasn't Beatrice.

When Bobby arrived, Sandeep's apartment was swarming with the usual crew of crime scene investigators. The coroner was gone, as was the body, but the detective in charge of the case was still on site and Rocky stood talking to him.

"Good morning, Burns." Inspector Armstrong was making some notes on his phone and only gave a quick nod to his fellow inspector.

"Hey, Armstrong. What have we got here so far?"

"Well, so far, a dead guy and not much else. Coroner says probably poison, cyanide, but whoever did it cleaned the scene up pretty good. No food or drink, just his and his roommates' fingerprints, no security or doorbell cameras. Doesn't look like suicide since everything was cleaned up after. What's your connection to the victim?"

"He was looking to be the prime suspect in my case. I guess he still could have killed Ms. Gardner, but it kind of puts him out of reach, for now."

"What's your girlfriend here for?"

Rocky did not look pleased at his reference. "I, Inspector Stafford of SFPD Fraud, am here because the vic was the center of a major case I'm working on."

Again, unimpressed, Armstrong did not look up from his phone. "Looks like somebody got to your guy before you did."

"We'd like to take a look at his room. Were his computer and phone here?"

"Yes on the phone and computer; we've already booked them into evidence.

Rocky and Bobby walked through the apartment sidestepping the crime scene crew. Everything looked just like you'd expect to see an apartment with three guys living in it, plus the fingerprint powder, rifled drawers and cabinets, and the usual litter.

On the way out Bobby said, "Can you make sure I get copied on all the reports on this? I need to see if I have two murders by the same perp, or two separate killers."

"I think this case should be transferred to you and Stafford. My plate's pretty full." Armstrong finally looked interested.

"We'll see what shakes out later today."

Down on the street Bobby walked Rocky to her car. She still looked miffed at Armstrong. "Let it go, he's just an asshole."

"Tell me about it." She shrugged and opened her car door. "I wonder who gets all the foundation money now, including the money your victim left him. My next stop is the attorney on Van Ness."

"I'm going to go see the coroner, maybe pick up Morris. She could use some field experience."

"How is she doing anyway? I hear she's very efficient…"

"Hmmph."

CHAPTER FORTY-SEVEN

Dr. Kirschman, the coroner, was her usual bubbly self. "Surprised to see you here, Burns, this isn't your case, is it?"

"Not officially, but the guy was my best suspect in the Gardner thing. Scamming rich, sick, old ladies out of their money. Don't know what to think."

"Well, this is pretty straightforward. The guy ingested cyanide, possibly in food, more likely in wine. Was eating Indian food and keeled right over. It would have been fast."

"Must have been take-out since there was no sign of food or wine at the scene."

"Sounds like a possibility. Guy was late thirties, healthy, leaning to a bit of a beer gut."

"I am going to go talk to the electronics techs. They've had his computer since last night. Should have been able to get into it by now."

"Do you want to be copied on the report when it is finished?"

"Yeah, send it to Morris. It looks like it may be linked to my case and Inspector Stafford's fraud case; copy her on it, as well."

Dr. Kirschman had already turned back to her computer as Bobby left her office.

Bobby made the short walk to headquarters and found Morris still poring over videos. "Anything new?"

"Actually, there is a bit here that looks promising. I was just going to call you. Look here." Morris moved her chair aside and brought up another screen.

Bobby watched for a few moments before he saw a figure wearing a hoodie and dark glasses walk rapidly into view on a neighbor's camera. The person carried a small basket and walked out of sight to Greta's front door. About ten seconds later another, very recognizable figure entered the frame on the way to the entrance. Ms. Annabelle Leigh herself, although her hands were empty. She almost collided with the hoodie person as they left. "When was this taken?"

"A couple of weeks ago. On a Monday."

"Run it again. It looks like Ms. Leigh came in right behind the delivery person who had left the basket at the door. I'll need to talk to Ms. Campbell about any deliveries. Fortunately, I know right where she is. Come with me, Morris."

The young woman jumped to her feet. "Yes, sir…"

On the way to Annabelle's condo Bobby took a shot at getting to know the young officer better. "So, are you from the Bay Area?"

"Yes."

"Which part?"

"San Jose."

"Great, nice town…good hockey team. Soccer…"

The young woman stared straight ahead.

"I'm from the North Bay, San Rafael."

No response.

"What's your first name?"

"Barbie."

"Barbara?"

"No, just Barbie."

Finally, Bobby fell back on explaining where they were going. "The woman in the video, the older woman, not the delivery person, was in what looks like a purposeful hit-and-run accident a few days ago. She just got home from the hospital today and we need to know what she remembers about running into that delivery guy."

Still nothing from Morris.

"It's possible, maybe likely, that the poisoned bath stuff was in that basket. The woman who lived with the vic, Beatrice Campbell, is taking care of the woman in the video, so we can catch both of them at the same time to see what they remember."

Morris shifted slightly in her seat.

"Ms. Campbell mentioned a gift delivery, but didn't know who brought it"

Morris nodded.

Bobby pulled up in front of the condos on Fulton Street. Amazingly, there was a recently vacated parking spot. Some things were just meant to be.

Beatrice answered the door and ushered them into the now quite crowded living room.

Besides the hospital bed containing Ms. Leigh, Beatrice was there, and Kestrel Jonas and a short man Bobby had never seen before.

"Kestrel, I thought I told you to stay out of this. Who's your friend?"

"Bobby, this is Lester Stuyvesant. I am out of this. We just brought some of Beatrice's belongings that she'll need while she's staying here."

"Oh, Inspector Burns, it is quite lovely to have so much company, especially since Bertie just had dinner delivered to us. We have Chinese food for the masses here, and from the City View near Chinatown. Bertie told me he was dropping by with a surprise."

"Mr. Frankel is here, as well?"

"Oh, no. He just had the food delivered for us all. He'll probably stop by a bit later. Beatrice would you get us some plates and cutlery? There's enough for everyone here."

"I just need to ask you and Beatrice about a delivery Ms. Gardner received a couple of weeks ago. It was dropped off by a person wearing a hoodie and dark glasses. You came to Ms. Gardner's door just as they were leaving. Do you recall?"

"Of course, I recall it. They almost knocked me off the step. It was a gift basket wrapped in cellophane. It looked like it had candles and bath stuff in it."

"So, do you remember anything about the delivery person?"

"It was a woman, I think."

Bobby turned to Beatrice as she returned to the room with tableware. "Ms. Campbell, do you recall receiving a basket delivered to the Walnut

Street address?"

"Yes, I mentioned it to you before. It was a nice gift basket with some candles, incense, and bath bombs. It had a card with Greta's name on it but no signature. I showed it to Greta and she had me unpack it and place the items in her bathroom."

Just then the doorbell rang and Beatrice turned to answer it. "It's Mr. Frankel," she called as Bertie sauntered into the room.

"Oh my, it looks like I interrupted a party."

"Yes, it is a party, thanks to your generosity." Annabelle smiled.

"My generosity?"

"Yes, all this yummy Chinese food you had delivered. What a wonderful surprise."

Bertie looked at the groaning table of take-out boxes. "I didn't have any food delivered. I hate Chinese food."

It only took a few seconds for this news to sink into Bobby's consciousness. "Nobody eat anything. Has anybody eaten any of this food?"

Everyone looked at one another and the couple of people who had begun filling plates, put them down immediately.

"Morris, call the station and have a team come out here to gather this stuff up. Did anyone taste any of this food?" Everyone shook their heads.

"Inspector, what are you doing? If Bertie didn't have it sent, someone else must have. You are being ridiculous and frightening everyone." Annabelle had motioned for Beatrice to crank her bed into a better sitting position. "I'm sure there is nothing wrong with this food."

"Ms. Leigh, let me assure you that I am not being ridiculous. I have two bodies at the morgue, both of whom were poisoned. Do you want to take that risk?"

Turning to Beatrice he asked, "Did you answer the door when this was delivered?"

"No, the bell rang and when I went to answer it had been left on the doorstep."

"Do you have a doorbell camera?"

"Ms. Leigh can call it up on her phone."

"Ms. Leigh, would you please call up the video of the delivery?"

Annabelle scoffed in annoyance, but said, "Yes, let me just do that. There it is."

Bobby moved to her side to view the tape. After the bell was rung a figure had bent down to place the bags on the step. The person stood and then turned and went quickly down the steps and out of sight. But, for a few seconds she stared directly into the camera.

"That's the same person who delivered the basket to Greta. I recognize them, her." Suddenly Annabelle let out a strangled sound. "And I know where else I've seen her. That is the woman from the Finance office at UCSF. I knew I would remember where I'd seen her before." Her tone was triumphant.

"The woman from Finance? Do you remember her name?"

"Yes, of course. That is Sunita Khan, from the Finance office. I was on my way to meet with her when I had my accident."

"Are you certain that is her?"

Annabelle squinted at the video as she ran it over again. "Yes, I am sure."

Morris had stepped out of the room to call in a crime scene team and returned just as Bobby turned for the front door. "Morris, you're with me." Turning back to the people in the room, "Nobody touch any of that food. I don't need any more dead bodies."

CHAPTER FORTY-EIGHT

With rush hour traffic it took twenty minutes for Bobby and Morris to reach the Medical Center. Bobby snagged a relatively close parking spot.

The finance office was quiet at the end of the day, but it was not yet closed. A single woman sat at a front desk. Her nametag identified her only as Mary. "May I help you?" She looked a bit surprised to be getting visitors, as the finance office wasn't exactly a social hub.

"Yes, I'm Inspector Burns from SFPD and this is Sergeant Morris. We are looking for Sunita Khan."

"Well, this is the right office, but Ms. Khan called in sick today."

"Called in sick. Okay, well, I am going to need her home address."

"I can't give you that. It is private information."

"This is a police investigation and I don't have a lot of time to get the information."

"Well, I suppose I can give the police the information." Mary looked a little excited that the police were looking for Sunita. Too bad there weren't more people still in the office to see it. Never mind, she would spice the story up a bit when she retold it in the coffee room.

The woman tapped a few keys on the computer and wrote the address down on a sticky note for them.

"Thank you. Before we go, do you know or have you ever seen this man with Ms. Khan?" Bobby had pulled the photo of Sandeep up on his phone and showed the woman.

"I have never seen him in person, but his picture is on the desk in Ms. Khan's office, and in an expensive frame."

"Do you know who he is or how Ms. Khan knows him?"

"No, sir. I thought he was maybe her brother or someone. I don't think she has a boyfriend. She never talks about one."

"All right, well, thank you." Bobby turned away and then back to her. "Please don't call Ms. Khan and tell her that we are on our way."

"Oh, no. I won't."

On the way to Sunita's apartment Bobby tried to fill Morris in on what he was thinking. She didn't seem to be listening, and did not respond, but he did find it helped him to talk things through.

When they reached it, the apartment building was a bit of a surprise. In an older Art Deco–type building, the lobby was light and airy and had a posh feel to it. The apartment was on the third floor and Bobby took the stairs rather than wait for the older elevator.

Bobby wasn't sure what they would find at the apartment but was surprised when Sunita answered the door immediately. "May I help you?"

"Yes, Ms. Khan. I am Inspector Burns and this is Sergeant Morris of the San Francisco Police Department. May we come in?"

Sunita reached her hand out and held the edge of the ID Bobby flashed at her before stepping back and allowing them into the apartment.

The living room was not spacious and was dominated by an overly large television. The kitchen was immaculate and the doors to other rooms were closed.

"Do you know a man called Sandeep Sheik?"

"Yes, casually. He works at the university."

"I am not sure if you have heard but, he was found murdered on Sunday evening. Poisoned."

Sunita's only response was to raise an eyebrow. "That is very sad, but why are you telling me? I barely knew the man."

"That is surprising Ms. Khan, since the information we have is that you were involved in a non-profit foundation he established."

"Well, yes, but that was our only connection and it was strictly a business relationship."

"A business relationship that had you keeping a framed picture of him on your desk?"

"That was just there to prevent clients from trying to become too friendly with me. You know, so it would look like I was already involved with someone."

"So, you didn't have a more intimate relationship with him?"

Sunita laughed lightly. "Of course not. That is ludicrous, Inspector."

Now that Bobby had a chance to get a better look at the woman, he noted that she looked like she might be getting ready to go out. Her long, thick hair was arranged in an intricate braid and wrapped around her head. In the light he could see that a elaborate design of symbols and figures covered her lower arms and hands. "Has Mr. Sheik ever been to this apartment or have you been to his home?"

"He may have been here to sign papers, since our business relationship did not involve the university, but I have certainly never been to his apartment."

"Yet you know he lived in an apartment."

"Just a guess, Inspector. Almost everyone in San Francisco lives in an apartment." She smiled.

"I understand that you called in sick to your office today. Are you not feeling well?"

"I am feeling quite well. I just needed a day off to prepare for a wedding. My office mates don't need to know all my business. I almost never take any time off."

"But you are not leaving town are you? We may need to speak with you again."

"Oh, no. I am not going anywhere."

"Just to save some time, Sergeant Morris and I would like to look at your phone and look around your apartment."

"I'm sorry, but that won't be possible unless you have a warrant. It is quite intrusive unless you suspect me of some crime. Even then, you would need a warrant."

"But, if you have nothing to hide it would take us just a few minutes."

"I'm afraid I don't have a few minutes. In fact, this interview has taken far too much of my time. I need to continue my preparations."

Bobby considered trying to push the point, but decided he didn't really have much evidence against Sunita. Only that she knew the victim and was involved in his scam.

"The Shining Hope Foundation. You worked with Dr. Sheik on setting that up, is that correct?"

"Yes, but that was my only involvement with the man."

Bobby wondered for a moment if that were true. Could this be a business rivalry about money? "Did you have access to the financial records?"

"I know nothing about Mr. Sheik's finances, personal or otherwise. Now, I really must ask you to leave me. I am already going to be late with my preparations."

Bobby motioned Morris toward the door. "All right, but please don't make plans to leave the area in the next couple of days. We may well be back with a warrant."

"Oh, don't worry about me. I will be here when you come back. I'm not leaving the area, as you say."

Back in the car Bobby waited for a few minutes before heading out. "What was the deal with the tattoo things all over her hands, do you think?"

"That was ceremonial henna, like for weddings. She had it on her feet and legs, as well."

"Did she? I didn't notice."

"Yes, it is quite a big deal in many Indian weddings. It must have cost her like a thousand dollars, maybe more."

"But that's just for brides, right?"

"Sometimes, but all the women in the bridal party might have it done for a big wedding. They make a party of it."

Bobby just shook his head. A thousand bucks to get your hands and feet painted. What was that about? "Start the process for trying to get a warrant to search her apartment and electronics. There should be enough of a personal and business connection to push it through."

On the way back to the station Morris received a call. The Chinese food that Sunita Khan had delivered to Annabelle's condo contained enough cyanide to poison everyone who was there, including him and Morris. Sometimes you dodged a bullet when you didn't even know you were in the sights.

CHAPTER FORTY-NINE

As a matter of fact, the elaborate henna on Sunita's hands and feet had cost her well over a thousand dollars because she'd paid to have it done at the last minute.

She had spent the weekend having a manicure and pedicure, her eyebrows threaded, her hair braided and arranged. Those things had to be done right before the wedding, but the other preparations for the ceremony had been in the works for a very long time.

When the police had vacated her space she had gone into her bedroom, lit incense sticks and candles, and continued her preparations.

In the background, music from her favorite Bollywood films played. She'd always loved the joy and romance of Indian film. She'd watched many of them again and again as a teen and still kept a library of DVDs in her closet. Of course, she had never shared those with Sandeep. He'd have laughed at her, but in her dreams she was still the beautiful heroine whose love and virtue would triumph in the end, usually with an exuberant dance finale, including elephants, bright colors, and joyous singing.

On the bed she had arranged her blood-red lehenga choli. The circular ankle-length skirt was heavy with gold embroidery, as was the choli top. The deep red color of the garments represented the depth of her love. She'd bought this dress when she first started seeing Sandeep. She'd told herself that she was just preparing for her future marriage. She had been sure, after all that she had done for him, he would eventually marry her.

The young women at the shop in Berkeley had helped her pick the perfect outfit, and their laughter and sly comments as she told them of her upcoming wedding had buoyed her dreams.

On the dresser she had arranged her makeup and her cache of gold jewelry, accumulated since her mother began investing in her future when she was eight years old. The bangles, earrings, necklaces, anklets, and rings represented her tangible worth. It was a part of what she would bring to a marriage and also what would protect her in dark times when she could pawn or sell it, if needed, to save herself or to support her family. Today, she would wear most of it, the weight and gleam of it reminding her of her worth.

Usually, a bride would have family members to help her dress in the heavy skirt and drape the flowing dupatta perfectly, but she would have to do this herself. She did not rush, as the donning of each garment and piece of jewelry had special meaning to her. The music played in the background and she sang along with it: *"Sabko na kar di tujhko haan kar di/Main jaana tere sang sohneya"* (I said no to everyone and I said yes to you/I want to go with you).

When she was ready she turned the music up and entered the living room she had decorated with candles and flowers. A picture of Sandeep had place of honor in a golden frame draped with a marigold garland. The blinds were opened on the setting sun and the scent of the incense, flowers, and candles was overpowering.

She walked to the window and poured a glass of champagne. A tiny golden bowl containing white powder stood before Sandeep's photo and she gently tipped it up, watching the crystals swirl into the bubbly liquid in her glass.

The music was very loud and she knew her neighbors would be complaining soon, but it was not hers to worry about. Someone else would have to turn down the music.

As she raised the glass she thought she heard a voice calling her name, again and again. She was probably imagining it, but she let herself believe for a moment that it was her groom beckoning her. She raised her glass to her bridegroom and holding it in both hands she brought it to her lips.

Bobby had asked Morris to call and expedite a search warrant before they even got back to the station. "Make sure it includes finding and searching her car. I think she's the one that ran down the Leigh woman, too."

"It all seems to fit, but there's something else going on."

This was the first time Bobby had heard Morris utter an entire sentence. "What else is going on?"

"Well, she's just super-calm and accepting. She isn't worried about us, at all."

"Crooks are always like that. They think they are so smart that nobody will ever catch them, and they are never as smart as they think they are."

"Maybe…" But Morris didn't sound convinced.

They were almost back to the station when she spoke again. "You know, I don't think she is going to a wedding. At least not someone else's wedding."

"It doesn't really matter where she says she is going as long as we get back there before she can leave."

"That's what I mean, I don't think she is going anywhere."

"But what about all the painted hands and flowers, and all?"

"You have all those things in a wedding, but not everyone gets hennaed and prepared like that. It's usually the bridal couple that are going all out."

"You mean you think she's getting married? After killing an old lady and her boyfriend, and trying to off another old lady, she's just going to go get married?"

"No, Detective Burns, what I am saying is, she is preparing for a wedding, preparing to meet her groom, preparing to die."

"Kill herself? What good will that do?"

It was a good thing that Bobby was not good at reading women's minds or he'd be frizzled into a cowering ball by the look that Morris gave him. "I think that she is going to kill herself, and we have just gone away and let her do it."

Bobby stopped dead at the entrance of the elevator, letting the mass of riders move around him. As the doors were about to close he turned on his heel and headed back out the door. "We have to go back, even without the search warrant."

Morris followed him obediently and, when they reached the apartment building she followed him up the stairs, not waiting for the creaky elevator to fetch them. As they got near they could hear joyful music.

Bobby knocked on the door, then knocked again. He pounded on the door and shouted her name. "Sunita, Sunita Khan. This is the police. Open the door… Sunita."

By the time Bobby decided he'd have to try knocking down the door Morris had already dialed 9-1-1. She told the operator the address and that it was a suspected cyanide poisoning.

Doors are not nearly as easy to knock down as television would lead you to believe. In a city like San Francisco in the twenty-first century, even interior doors are solid.

After several tries he turned to see that Morris had kicked in the fire extinguisher case and held the heavy canister out to him. He took it and used it to bash the handle off the door.

By then he could already hear sirens approaching as he burst through the door and found Sunita sprawled on the carpet in front of the window. The picture of Sandeep had been knocked askew and she was unconscious, covered in red silk and golden bangles. The suffocating smoke of incense swirled around the room. "Turn off that damned music." Morris quickly complied.

CHAPTER FIFTY

It was late when Bobby finally drove away from the station. The marine layer had slid in to blanket the city and a fine sheen of moisture coated the windshield. He didn't even know where he was going. He could go home or he could drive to Rocky's place. It was late, but he thought she might still be awake waiting to hear from him.

He should call, at least, but he didn't have the energy. He didn't know what to say.

Sunita Khan was either very lucky, or very unlucky; he couldn't decide which. She had balked at the last moment and not drunk the entire glass of poisoned champagne. Most of it had ended up dribbled down the front of her elaborate gown.

The first responders had been the fire department who carried a cyanide antidote kit they were testing out. Most people get a cyanide dose from burning materials, and many of them are firefighters. So, who better to be able to treat it?

The "bride" had been hauled away to the hospital and she might even survive. She was unconscious so he'd let the medics take care of her while he and Morris searched the apartment.

Morris had been able to identify the items stored in the bottom of the closet as the materials used to make bath bombs: citric acid, salt, bicarbonate of soda, essential oils, and in this case, a partial vial of cyanide. Sunita had drawn on her chemistry degree to aid her in safely packaging the cakes of powder into balls; and wrapping them in plastic and netting, tying them with ribbons, embellishing them with tiny sprigs of lavender. They found instructions for making incense cones as well as disposable gloves and a respirator half mask and goggles for working with chemicals.

When they were able to get access to the parking garage for the apartment complex they found that the front of Sunita's car had been damaged and that part of what Morris claimed was an Hermès scarf hung from the bumper. Bobby would have to take her word on that.

Among the items they found was a legal-sized file folder containing the "résumé" and photos of the ever-so-suitable bride that Sandeep's parents had chosen for him. It included her name, age, education, parents' details, occupation, mobile, email address, height, birthplace, birth time, *gotra* (lineage), caste, and sibling details. Sunita must have removed it from Sandeep's apartment.

Bobby had been surprised at the level of Morris's knowledge of Indian bridal customs and bath-bomb making. She was turning out to be a surprising resource for things he'd never thought he needed to know.

Bobby circled the block of Rocky's apartment building several times, craning his neck to see whether he could detect light in any of her windows.

Rocky had been dozing on the couch when she heard the knock and she rushed to answer the door. "Hey, stranger, looks like you've had a long day."

"Yes, a long and ugly day."

"Well, guess what, I can help with that. I've got beer, sandwich stuff, Oreos, whatever you could want, and you can tell me, or not tell me, anything. Come on in."

Instead, Bobby reached out to bring her into a bear hug. "I am so glad to be home."

CHAPTER FIFTY-ONE

Kestrel hesitated only a moment before she pushed the button sending her latest blog post out. This particular update had been harder to write than many. So many pieces had fallen into place in the past few days.

Sunita Khan was going to live, though the long-term affects to her heart and nervous system were still unclear. Sandeep Sheik's parents had arrived from India and were demanding that any mention of the Shining Hope Foundation be struck from all records.

It had been especially difficult to disclose everything she'd found out without giving away her identity. After all, who but she would know all of the bits and pieces, even to the detailed description of Sunita's suicide attempt that her latest minion, Sargeant Barbie Morris, had disclosed.

The Memorial for Greta Gardner had been arranged by her dear friends, Annabelle Leigh and Bertram Frankel, and it looked like it would be the social event of the usually dull post-holiday season.

It was discouraging that so many dirty dealings and plans would be, as usual, swept under the rug. She reminded herself that this was why she needed to keep publishing her blog.

ABOUT THE AUTHOR

Lexa M. Mack is an avid mystery reader and writer who lives with her husband, a very fat cat, five chickens, and forty thousand honeybees in the Sierras near South Lake Tahoe. She spends her days blogging about the surprises of retirement and dreaming up creative ways to murder people.

Made in the USA
Las Vegas, NV
17 November 2024